The Touch You Can't Feel

OrangeBooks Publication

1st Floor, Rajhans Arcade, Mall Road, Kohka, Bhilai, Chhattisgarh 490020

Website: **www.orangebooks.in**

First Edition, 2026

ISBN: 978-93-7426-545-1

Price: Rs. 350.00

Printed in India

The Touch You Can't Feel

Where feelings exist without form

Leekshith

OrangeBooks Publication
www.orangebooks.in

Foreword

I first read Lee's story as a set of late-night drafts—scenes written in bursts, characters arriving like shadows, and emotions that refused to stay quiet. The pages were not polished at the beginning. They weren't trying to impress anyone. They were trying to survive.

What struck me immediately was not the scale of the plot, but the honesty behind it. This is a novel that doesn't pretend the world is fair. It doesn't soften darkness to make it easier to digest. Instead, it asks a harder question: *What happens to people who carry guilt, grief, and unfinished truth—and how far will they go to face it?*

As the manuscript grew, I watched the story transform into something more structured, more deliberate. Lee became more than a man with wealth and discipline—he became a person shaped by the cost of change. Akshara became more than a ghost—she became memory given motion, justice given voice, and pain given a purpose. Even in the supernatural elements, the book stays rooted in something painfully real: the consequences of silence, and the damage caused when power is allowed to operate unchecked.

This story is not written to comfort you.

It is written to hold your attention, test your emotions, and leave you thinking after the final page.

If you're opening this book expecting an easy mystery, you may be surprised by how personal it becomes. But if you're opening it prepared for a journey through grief, loyalty, and the search for truth—then you're exactly where you need to be

Preface

His book began as a single scene in my mind—one moment, one place, one feeling that refused to leave me. I didn't start with a perfect plot or a full outline. I started with a question:

What if someone who never got justice came back—not to haunt the world, but to understand it?

At first, I wrote without worrying about structure. I focused on emotions, atmosphere, and the weight of silence that follows tragedy. As the chapters grew, the story became clearer. Lee's life took shape as a man who looks strong from the outside but carries a past that shaped him in ways no one sees. Akshara's journey became more than a ghost story—it became an investigation, a confrontation, and a search for closure that goes beyond death.

While writing, I wanted to mix realism with the supernatural. The locations are familiar—Hyderabad, hospitals, crowded roads, forgotten forests—because the darkest truths don't always happen in distant places. Sometimes they happen in the most normal streets, hidden behind routines and power.

This story is also about transformation:

How people change, how guilt becomes responsibility, how love can survive even when it cannot stay the same.

I hope you feel the tension, the mystery, and the emotion exactly the way I felt it while writing.

Thank you for reading.

— T.Leekshith Reddy

Introduction

Some stories are written to entertain.

This one is written to uncover what people bury.

At its heart, this novel is a supernatural investigation—one man and one restless spirit searching for the truth behind a death that was never properly recorded, never properly answered, and never properly forgiven. But as the mystery deepens, the story becomes more than a hunt for clues. It becomes a journey through grief, guilt, justice, and the consequences of power.

This book explores three things:

- **How truth can disappear** when the system itself chooses silence.
- **How love can exist in complicated forms**—as loyalty, regret, sacrifice, and unfinished promises.
- **How darkness changes people**, and what it takes to fight it without becoming part of it.

If you've ever wondered what justice looks like when the world refuses to provide it—this story is for you.

And if you believe that some souls don't return to scare the living…

But to demand answers—

Then welcome.

Table of Contents

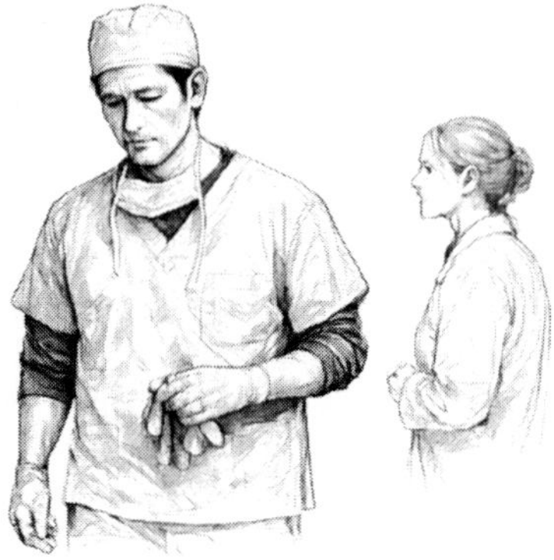

Chapter - 1
Rushing Hours

Sunday, December 28, 2025

Winter came quietly to Hyderabad, almost apologetically. The city was unaccustomed to cold that lingered—cold that crept rather than struck. That morning, it lay wrapped in a thin, unfamiliar hush, as though the city itself had paused mid-breath.

At 7:30 a.m., the streets below Dr. Lee's apartment were unusually subdued. The early vendors had not yet raised their voices. Even the stray dogs that normally claimed the footpaths were curled tightly into themselves, conserving warmth. A pale winter sun hovered behind a veil of clouds, offering light without comfort.

Inside the apartment, silence reigned.

Dr. Lee woke abruptly.

There was no gradual return to consciousness, no lazy stretch or lingering thought. His eyes opened sharply, alert before his body fully followed. They moved instantly to the digital clock beside his bed.

7:30.

For a moment, the numbers made no sense. His mind rejected them outright, insisting there had been a mistake—an error in perception, a trick of half-sleep.

Then his heart reacted.

A sudden, violent jolt struck his chest, sharp enough to steal breath. The calm of the room shattered in that instant.

The alarm should have rung at six.

It always rang at six.

For years—without exception—it had rung at six.

Order was not something Dr. Lee admired. It was something he depended on. Routine held his life together in ways emotion never could. When routine failed, something far deeper than inconvenience was threatened.

He sat upright immediately, the warmth of the blanket slipping away unnoticed. Cold air brushed his skin, invasive and sharp. A faint pressure settled behind his sternum—not panic, not fear, but a persistent unease that refused to name itself.

No phone calls.

No blinking notifications.

Yet instinct—honed through countless emergencies, long nights, and losses he never allowed himself to revisit—told him something had already gone wrong.

He moved through the apartment with practiced efficiency.

The place was spotless, minimal, almost clinical. Everything had a position. Everything remained untouched unless necessary. He preferred it that way. Disorder invited thought, and thought invited memory.

The silence followed him from room to room, heavier than usual. The apartment was always quiet—too quiet for a man who lived alone—but that morning it felt different. As though it was not empty, but waiting.

He dressed without hesitation.

A light blue formal shirt, crisp and cool against his skin. Charcoal-grey tailored trousers, pressed sharply enough to cut reflection. Polished black shoes slipped on without effort. He paused only briefly before pulling a thin woolen sweater over the shirt—not for warmth, but acknowledgment. Winter demanded respect, even if it offered none in return.

The mirror reflected a man in control.

Clean-shaven. Hair neatly combed. Shoulders straight, posture disciplined. He looked as he always did—calm, composed, reliable.

Only his eyes betrayed him.

They were darker than usual, focused yet distant, as though searching for something he could not yet see.

Outside, the cold struck immediately.

The winter air was dry and biting, slipping into lungs without invitation. Even inside the car, with the heater humming softly, the cold persisted—threading itself through vents, clinging to skin, refusing comfort. It felt deliberate, as though the morning itself wished to remind him that discipline did not make one immune.

He drove.

By 7:40 a.m., Hyderabad had begun to stir.

Traffic thickened quickly, indifferent to urgency or profession. Auto horns flared impatiently. Buses braked sharply, coughing smoke into the air. Motorcycles darted through impossible gaps, unconcerned with consequence. The city moved on its own terms, unmoved by the lives that depended on minutes.

Every red signal felt personal.

Each delay tightened something inside him. His fingers tapped lightly against the steering wheel as he checked the dashboard clock again and again, calculating distances, rehearsing explanations he hoped he would never need to offer.

Ten minutes, he thought grimly.

I should have been there in ten minutes.

But the city disagreed.

At 7:50 a.m., the hospital finally emerged from the traffic—concrete, glass, order.

He slowed instinctively.

And then he saw it.

An ambulance turned sharply into the emergency entrance, its siren slicing cleanly through the cold morning air. The sound was sharp, commanding, unmistakable.

Relief flooded him.

Not carelessly.

Not completely.

But undeniably.

He was not too late.

By 8:00 a.m., Dr. Lee had parked, authenticated his identity, and moved through the corridors with the ease of someone who belonged there. The scent of antiseptic settled into his senses, familiar and grounding. Footsteps echoed crisply against polished floors. Voices carried urgency without chaos.

The hospital functioned on order.

Unlike the city outside.

Though officially designated a general surgeon, Dr. Lee's skill reached far beyond labels. Over the years, he had immersed himself deeply in orthopedics—observing senior specialists, assisting whenever permitted, learning when others chose rest. Curiosity had evolved into competence, and competence into quiet authority.

Medicine, to him, was not a profession bound by specialization.

It was responsibility.

Inside the operation theater, time dissolved.

There was only movement—controlled, deliberate. Instructions were short, precise. Every incision carried weight. Every pause meant calculation. The outside world ceased to exist, replaced by the measured rhythm of focus.

By 10:15 a.m., it was done.

Successful.

As he stepped out, removing his gloves, Dr. Alena approached him. Relief softened her face, tension finally loosening from her shoulders.

"Congratulations, sir," she said. "The operation went perfectly."

He acknowledged her with a small nod and a restrained smile. Praise had long lost its power over him. Outcome was all that mattered.

Later, in the canteen, steam rose from steel cups as Alena spoke—cases, doubts, unresolved questions. Dr. Lee answered patiently, his tone calm and distant. He inspired trust without inviting closeness.

Then she asked the question she always carried.

"You're wealthy enough to build a hospital larger than this," she said softly. "Yet you choose to work here… and live alone. Why?"

He paused.

"When you lose something you worked very hard for," he said quietly, "the result of that hard work begins to feel meaningless."

She did not ask again.

That evening, as winter light faded, Dr. Lee drove toward the other life he never spoke about.

Some lives were built in applause.

Others, in quiet service.

And some mornings—cold, delayed, and unforgiving—stood unknowingly at the edge of something far darker yet to come.

Chapter - 2
Long Ago

PUTRI

Sunday, December 28, 2025 — 9:00 P.M.

The nights in the Nallamala forest were not simply dark. They were ancient.

Darkness there did not fall like a curtain—it arrived like a decision. It settled in layers, thick and deliberate, as though the forest itself chose what could be seen and what must remain hidden. Even the air felt older, carrying dampness from centuries of rain and rot, carrying the smell of soil, fallen leaves, moss—and beneath it all, something metallic that did not belong.

The last pilgrims had long descended from the mountain temple of Vidudhala. By day, the peak belonged to devotion—bells ringing softly, incense curling skyward, prayers rising in steady chants as bare feet climbed worn stone steps toward Hanuman's shrine. Faith filled the paths in sunlight.

But by night, the mountain belonged to something else.

Something that existed long before temples were built.

The forest knew it.

Trees leaned inward as the road narrowed, their trunks tall and dark, bark scarred by time. Teak and bamboo stood close together like silent sentries, their branches interlocking high above in a canopy so dense the moonlight could barely press through. When it did, it broke into thin fragments—pale and trembling—touching only patches of ground before being swallowed again.

Mist clung low to the earth, sliding across roots like breath. The road wound unnaturally, forced to curve around thick coils of roots that rose like sleeping serpents. Stones glistened with moisture, reflecting faintly in the truck's headlights like half-open eyes.

At 9:00 p.m., a truck moved slowly through that narrow path.

Its engine hummed low, restrained, almost respectful—as if even the machine sensed the territory it had entered. The headlights sliced forward in thin, wavering beams. Dust rose briefly behind the tires and then fell again, smothered by dampness and night.

The truck carried no ordinary cargo.

The back was stacked with wooden crates—hundreds of them—bound tight with rope and reinforced with iron strips. Inside each crate were glass bottles packed shoulder-to-shoulder, clinking softly whenever the truck hit uneven ground.

But the clinking was not the strangest sound.

It was the glow.

Each bottle shimmered faintly from within. Light leaked through cracks between crates, painting the road and tree trunks in colors that did not belong to nature. Blue. Green. Violet. Yellow. Their hues shifted restlessly, as though they were alive, as though what was trapped inside them did not sleep.

Auras pressed against the glass like breath trapped in a sealed mouth.

They pulsed in irregular rhythms—expanding, contracting—as if the bottles were lungs and the lights inside them were forced to inhale and exhale without ever escaping.

The forest reacted immediately.

A spotted deer froze between trees, its body rigid, ears twitching violently as it sensed the unnatural glow passing through its home. A langur leapt across branches overhead, its silhouette sharp for a heartbeat before vanishing into shadow, leaving behind a warning cry. Somewhere deeper, an owl shifted on its perch, wings adjusting without sound, gaze fixed unblinkingly on the moving light.

Then the insects fell silent.

Crickets stopped mid-song. Cicadas withdrew as if a signal had passed through them. Even the wind seemed to hesitate, retreating into stillness, refusing to touch what traveled beneath the canopy.

Inside the cabin, the driver did not speak.

His hands were locked around the steering wheel, knuckles pale, veins raised like cords. His eyes stayed fixed on the road ahead with the rigid focus of a man afraid that looking away—even for a second—might invite something into the vehicle.

He did not glance at the cargo.

He did not glance at the man beside him.

Beside him sat Putri.

The leader of the Aghoris wore saffron—a clean pancha wrapped neatly at his waist and a saffron scarf resting loosely around his neck. The cloth looked untouched by dust, untouched by sweat, untouched by the ordinary burdens of travel. In the forest's darkness, the color did not fade.

It burned.

Putri sat perfectly still, spine straight, shoulders relaxed, posture heavy—not tense like the driver's, but inevitable. His face held no devotion, no fear, no anticipation. It was as though feeling itself had been removed long ago, discarded like an old skin.

In his right hand he held a single glass bottle, separate from the rest.

Unlike the other bottles, which glowed in wandering colors, this one burned crimson.

The red inside it was deeper than blood, darker than fire. It did not merely glow—it bled. Light spilled over his fingers, crawling slowly up his wrist like living heat, as if the aura recognized flesh and wanted more of it.

Putri did not react.

Outside, the forest recoiled.

A wild boar burst through bushes to the left, crashing blindly through undergrowth, driven by terror rather than direction. Behind the truck, monkeys screamed and scattered, branches whipping violently as they abandoned the road above. Birds exploded from the canopy in sudden frantic storms of wings. The world around the truck behaved like prey.

The man seated behind Putri—new to this journey—could no longer endure the silence.

"Where are we going?" he asked.

His voice sounded thin. Fragile. It was swallowed almost immediately by the night.

Putri did not turn his head.

"To the cave beneath the mountain," he replied, calm as breath. "Directly below the feet of Lord Hanuman's temple."

The man swallowed. His throat looked as though it hurt to move.

"And… what happens there?"

Putri's fingers tightened—barely, almost imperceptibly—around the crimson bottle.

“Every twenty-five years,” Putri said, voice steady, “a man from the Himalayas arrives at that place.”

The truck rolled onward, tires crunching softly over dead leaves and twigs.

“A rishi,” Putri continued, “whose origins trace back to the age of the Ramayana.”

A distant peacock cried—long, sorrowful—utterly wrong in the dead of night.

“When the time comes,” Putri said, “Hanuman enters his body.”

The man’s breath caught. “Hanuman… enters him?”

Putri’s gaze remained forward. His face remained empty.

“For two days,” he said, “Hanuman resides within the rishi and consumes every soul we carry. Every ghost. Every fragment of negative aura.”

He paused, letting the words settle like stones.

“Nothing survives.”

The man whispered, “Why him?”

Putri finally turned his eyes toward him.

They were calm.

Empty.

Ancient.

“Long ago,” Putri said, “a village was destroyed by spirits and malignant forces. The dead did not rest. The living were hunted.”

His voice lowered slightly—not with emotion, but with the weight of memory that did not belong to one lifetime.

“The rishi prayed without rest. Without fear. Without thought of death. Hanuman answered.”

Putri looked ahead once more, as if the forest demanded his attention.

"**Hanuman said:** I will remain within you for two days, once every twenty-five years, and I will cleanse this world of what should not exist."

The man swallowed again. "But spirits escape."

"They used to," Putri replied.

He gestured toward the road and the trees leaning inward—bark scarred, twisted, as though the forest itself carried old wounds.

"Hanuman created a pond," Putri said. "Without depth. Without boundary. From it came these vessels."

The man's gaze flicked toward the cargo.

One bottle rattled softly, vibrating as if it sensed something unseen traveling alongside them in the darkness.

"Any ghost sensed near them is drawn in," Putri said. "The aura is trapped. The pond has no limit."

The man hesitated, voice lowering. "And… how does the rishi arrive here?"

Putri raised the crimson bottle slightly.

Instantly, the glow intensified.

Red flooded the cabin. It spilled across the windshield, crept along the road, climbed the nearest trees. Shadows fled. Birds erupted again, frantic and blind. Even the mist seemed to recoil, pulling away from the light like skin shrinking from flame.

"When Hanuman enters his body," Putri said quietly, "there is no need for transport."

The road curved sharply.

Stone met earth.

Somewhere ahead, beneath the sacred mountain, the cave waited.

And the bottle in Putri's hand burned brighter still.

Chapter - 3
The Party

LEE

Thursday, December 31, 2025 — 9:30 P.M. to 12:15 A.M.

New Year's Eve had always belonged to them.

Not because the calendar demanded it, but because they did. Because it had become their ritual—an annual proof that life had not broken them, that time had not scattered them beyond return.

At 9:30 p.m., the rooftop of the sprawling city mall looked out over Hyderabad like a throne above a kingdom of lights. Glass towers reflected neon streaks. Traffic flowed below like glowing veins. Music thundered across the open terrace—deep bass, fast beats—vibrating through the floor and up into bone.

Winter wind moved gently at that height, cool against skin, carrying the scent of smoke from early fireworks and the sweet bite of perfume and alcohol. The air tasted like celebration—sharp, restless, alive.

The group had gathered near the center of the rooftop where lights hung overhead like stars made by men. Tables were lined with drinks, laughter spilling freely, glasses clinking, bodies moving without hesitation.

For most people, it was simply another party.

For Avaneesh, it was memory.

Their party had been hosted every year without fail—less a celebration of midnight and more a quiet acknowledgment of survival. Once they had been young men with cramped rooms, rationed meals, and ambition that outweighed sense. Now, the city around them stood as evidence.

Medicine. Information technology. Restaurants with branches across India. Clothing brands that crossed state lines. Construction firms that reshaped skylines.

And the mall itself—alive, thriving, overflowing.

All of it had begun under Lee's vision.

And yet not a single company publicly bore Lee's name.

That, too, was intentional.

Lee arrived dressed as he always did when he entered crowds: composed, precise, unreadable.

A tailored black blazer sat perfectly on his shoulders. Beneath it, a dark grey shirt—collar open, no tie—made him look effortless while hiding discipline. His watch was simple, expensive only to those who understood craftsmanship. His hair was neatly styled, his face clean-shaven, his expression calm enough to be mistaken for peace.

But Avaneesh knew better.

Avaneesh stood near the glass railing, one hand resting against it as he watched the party unfold. Of all of them, he was closest to Lee—not just in years of friendship, but in shared silences that required no explanation.

Or so he believed.

By tradition, they gathered every December 31st.

And by another tradition—one that never changed—Lee did not drink that night.

Never on the thirty-first.

Lee only drank on the night of January 1st.

Whenever someone teased him, Lee offered the same line, with that easy smile that made people accept without thought.

"Someone in the group should remain sober. Just in case of an emergency."

Everyone laughed.

Everyone accepted it.

Everyone except Avaneesh.

He had known Lee too long to believe in coincidences. Too long to mistake habit for chance.

The party rose like a wave.

By 11:00 p.m., the rooftop was crowded, music louder, laughter sharper. People danced without restraint, shouted into each other's ears, clapped to rhythms that rattled the glass railing. Fireworks began to pop across the horizon in premature impatience, scattering bursts of gold and crimson like impatient gods.

Lee stayed among them, smiling when spoken to, laughing when expected to. He offered toasts with water instead of alcohol. His movements were smooth, controlled. If anyone watched him casually, they would see a man present and relaxed.

But Avaneesh watched differently.

And he saw what the others did not.

Lee's eyes wandered.

Every year it was the same.

Three days before the New Year. Three days after. During that narrow stretch, Lee was never entirely himself. Something inside him withdrew, retreating behind discipline and composure. His laughter arrived a second too late. His silences lasted a second too long.

He drifted toward edges—balconies, windows, darker corners where the noise dulled into distant echo. Places where celebration could not reach fully.

Tonight was no different.

At 11:55 p.m., as the countdown began to roll through speakers, Lee stepped away from the crowd as if pulled by an invisible thread. He moved toward the railing, placing himself where the city's lights spread endlessly below.

Avaneesh followed at a distance.

The final minutes of the year stretched thin.

Voices rose around them: "Ten… nine… eight…"

Fireworks began to rise, painting the sky in violent color—gold, white, crimson—bursting and fading like brilliant promises that lasted only seconds.

Lee did not look up.

His gaze was fixed far beyond the skyline.

Beyond the city.

Beyond the year ending.

Avaneesh followed the line of his sight, but there was nothing there—only darkness stretched thin by distant lights.

What are you remembering? Avaneesh wondered.

The crowd roared as midnight struck.

12:00 a.m.

Cheers exploded. Drinks were thrown upward. Strangers hugged like old friends. Music surged.

Hyderabad welcomed a new year with fire and noise.

Lee stood still.

Unmoving.

Not celebrating.

Not mourning.

Just… present in a silence no one else could hear.

For everyone else, it was a beginning.

For Lee, it was always something else entirely.

By 12:15 a.m., the party continued behind them—louder, freer—but Avaneesh remained near the railing, watching Lee's face as fireworks faded into smoke.

Lee's expression never changed.

Yet Avaneesh felt it—like cold air slipping through sealed glass—

Tonight was not simply a tradition.

Tonight was a warning.

Chapter - 4
The Release

PUTRI

Friday, January 1 — 7:00 P.M.

Dusk settled heavily over the Nallamala forest.

The winter air was cold but still, carrying the scent of damp earth and ancient stone. A thin mist crept between trees, coiling around roots and fallen leaves like breath escaping unseen mouths. Above, the sky darkened into a muted indigo, the last traces of sunlight dissolving behind the mountain temple.

The ritual began with disciplined precision.

One by one, the glass jars were removed from the truck and carried into the depths of the cave. Each jar was wrapped in coarse cloth, held firmly against the chest, as though even a careless breath might provoke what lay trapped within. The Aghoris wore simple saffron pancha cloths, their torsos bare despite the cold, ash markings faint against their skin. Their bare feet echoed softly against the ancient stone floor as they moved inward, shadows stretching and folding along the cave walls.

No chants were spoken.

No prayers offered.

This was not faith.

This was responsibility.

At the heart of the cave lay the pond.

It had no visible edge.

No surface.

No reflection.

It was not water as the world understood it. It was presence—formless, boundless, unseen. The air around it felt colder, heavier, as though the cave itself bowed inward toward something immeasurable.

The moment a jar crossed the invisible threshold, the aura inside responded. Violent motion slowed. Frenzied colors dimmed. Resistance dissolved into surrender as each spirit was drawn toward a force infinitely older and stronger than itself.

When the final jar was placed, the cave seemed to exhale.

A count was taken.

Every vessel accounted for.

Or so it appeared.

Outside, the truck engine roared to life, shattering the forest's stillness for a brief moment before fading into the vastness of night. Putri stood at the cave entrance, his saffron cloth unmoving in the cold air, watching until even the memory of sound disappeared.

Only then did he speak.

"Check everything," he said calmly. "The jars. The ground. The walls. If even one breaks, the pond is too far to reclaim what escapes."

The Aghoris returned inside immediately, movements sharper now, tension tightening their shoulders. Fingers traced glass for cracks. Palms pressed against stone walls, listening for whispers beneath the rock.

Putri did not follow.

Unnoticed, he stepped away from the cave mouth, where the forest waited.

From within the folds of his cloth bag, he withdrew the final jar.

The forest reacted instantly.

Leaves trembled without wind. Cicadas that had screamed endlessly through the evening fell into sudden, unnatural silence. Somewhere deep within the trees, a deer cried out and fled blindly through the undergrowth. Birds burst from the canopy in frantic waves, wings beating wildly as though fleeing an unseen predator.

Inside the cave, the Aghoris froze.

Something was wrong.

The glass burned Putri's skin.

His palms blistered, blackened at the center, as though scorched from within. Pain radiated up his arms, sharp and relentless. Yet his grip did not loosen.

Inside the jar, the aura burned crimson—violent, restless, dense with rage and grief that had never found release. It pulsed like a wounded heart, desperate and dangerous.

Slowly, deliberately, Putri lifted the jar.

He pressed it against the point between his eyebrows.

The world collapsed.

Sound vanished.

Light withdrew.

A void opened.

The cave shuddered.

Water began dripping faster from unseen cracks above, striking stone in frantic rhythm. Torches flared violently, their flames bending sideways as if dragged by breath that did not exist. One Aghori dropped his lamp; the fire died instantly as an icy wave tore through the chamber.

From the void, a form emerged.

A woman.

Her presence tore through the darkness like a wound. The red aura exploded outward, flooding the cave with crimson light. Shadows stretched unnaturally long, writhing against the walls. Outside, the forest erupted—monkeys screamed, snakes fled their burrows, insects scattered as though the earth itself rejected what had been unleashed.

Her scream carried unbearable pain—loss layered upon loss, memory sharpened into fury.

Yet she could not touch him.

Putri stood unmoving, saffron cloth fluttering faintly in a wind that did not exist.

“I know,” he said calmly. “You want the truth of your death. But you are drowning in rage.”

The Aghoris collapsed. Some fell to their knees, clutching their chests. Others pressed foreheads to stone, chanting desperately as the pressure crushed their breath.

“I cannot allow a spirit to escape,” Putri said. “That is the law I serve.”

The forest groaned.

Tree trunks creaked as though bending beneath invisible weight. Branches snapped, though the sky above remained clear.

Putri paused.

Then his voice softened.

“But when I see pain such as yours… I choose to bend that law.”

The crimson wavered.

"I consider you my child," he said quietly. "Do not take the life of anyone whose existence is bound to another."

The change began.

Crimson drained slowly, replaced by calm blue—deep, steady, restrained. Tremors ceased. Torches steadied. Outside, animals fell silent—not in fear, but watchful stillness.

The jar slipped from Putri's hand.

It shattered.

From the broken glass, the blue aura escaped—silent, intentional—flowing into the forest and vanishing into the night.

Putri stood motionless.

The pond was too far.

And something released by compassion now walked free in a world unprepared for it.

Chapter - 5
The Meet

AKSHARA

Friday, January 1 — 7:30 P.M.

When Akshara crossed the boundary of the cave, the world struck her all at once.

Cold air rushed over her—sharp, dry, and unfamiliar. It cut through her presence like a blade through mist, carrying the scent of winter grass, distant smoke, and something metallic from the road beyond the forest. The Nallamala trees stood unnaturally still, their leaves barely stirring, as though the forest itself had not yet decided whether to accept her release.

The sky above was clear, washed in deep blue-black, stars scattered like indifferent witnesses.

It was January 1, 2026.

The understanding did not arrive as a single realization. It unfolded slowly, painfully, like frost creeping across glass. Roads felt wider than they should have been. Electric lights burned brighter, colder. Even the silence between sounds felt different—thinner, faster, impatient.

Time had not waited.

It had moved forward relentlessly while she had remained trapped in stillness.

The truth settled heavily into her awareness.

She was no longer part of the world she had died in.

Her first thought was Kiran.

The name surfaced instinctively, carrying warmth and ache together. She did not know where life had taken him, nor what time had shaped him into—but some habits endured beyond years. Every New Year, without fail, he went to his farmhouse with his college friends. It had been his ritual even when she was alive. Even when the future still felt negotiable.

She followed instinct more than memory.

The road leading to the farmhouse cut through open land, fields stretching wide beneath the winter night. Dry grass whispered softly in the breeze, bending and rising like breath. The farmhouse stood quietly beneath the fading evening sky, its windows glowing faintly with warm yellow light.

When she reached it, she saw him.

Kiran was older.

Time had softened him, carved restraint into his face. A neatly trimmed beard framed features that once carried careless laughter. He wore a dark sweater over a shirt, sleeves pushed up slightly, posture relaxed but heavy with responsibility. He sat with a few friends near the veranda, steel cups in hand, their voices low, their laughter subdued.

They spoke of college days—of cramped rooms, reckless nights, impossible dreams. Names surfaced of friends now scattered across continents. This year, many had not returned.

Akshara watched silently from the edge of the field.

Kiran smiled when he remembered, but sadness lingered behind his eyes like a shadow that refused to lift. This day still hurt him. The world believed she had died on January 1.

That was not true.

Even she did not know the exact moment her life had ended.

What she remembered clearly was the last day she lived—the last day she laughed freely, the last day she felt untouched by fear, by betrayal, by consequence.

Her thoughts were interrupted when Kiran's phone rang.

He stood, excused himself, and stepped inside his room. Alone, he answered the call and placed it on speaker.

"Happy New Year, Papa."

The words echoed softly against the walls.

Something twisted painfully inside her.

For a brief, fragile moment, she wondered if he had found peace. If time had finally eased the weight she left behind.

Then reality returned.

If any investigation began…

If anything went wrong…

If harm ever came to him—

His family would suffer.

She could not allow that.

She would not become the reason his life shattered again.

Something within her shifted.

Her aura deepened into calm blue—cool, observant, restrained. The anger she once carried dissolved into caution. Love demanded distance now, not presence.

She stepped back.

She left the farmhouse quietly, unseen, the winter wind swallowing her absence without question.

Lost, uncertain, and unwilling to involve anyone she loved, she made one final decision.

She would go to the place where she had died.

When she arrived, she barely recognized it.

What had once been a graveyard of silence and decay had transformed. Flowers bloomed across the ground in careful patterns, their colors vivid even beneath dim lights. Soft illumination shimmered through the space, glowing brighter as she stepped forward—as though the land itself recognized her presence.

The air there felt different. Still. Reverent.

And at the center of it all stood a man.

Lee.

He wore a dark coat, collar loosened, hair slightly disordered by wind and drink. A bottle hung loosely in his hand. His shoulders were slumped—not with exhaustion, but with something heavier.

He was drinking.

And he was crying.

She recognized him instantly.

Not just the man who had once confessed his love and been rejected.

He had been her closest friend before that.

Before awkward silences replaced laughter. Before distance grew where trust once lived.

A strange impulse stirred within her—gentle, mischievous, painfully familiar.

She decided to tease him.

Her aura shifted from blue to orange—warm, playful, alive.

Lee froze.

Fear seized him so suddenly that he staggered back, breath hitching as he turned and ran a few steps before stopping abruptly, as if his body no longer obeyed instinct.

She moved closer.

"Stop."

He did.

Standing beside him now, she asked softly, "What happened?"

Her gaze wandered over the place—the flowers, the lights, the care woven into every detail.

"Did you build all this… because of me?"

Lee's expression darkened.

He inhaled deeply before answering, anger rising quickly—not at her, but at himself.

"I don't buy land or build places because some girl rejected me," he said sharply. "That would make me weak. I built this place because I saw an opportunity. Someone sold it cheap because something bad happened here. That's all."

Akshara paused.

Understanding arrived quietly—and painfully.

He doesn't even know I died here.

And yet…

The care.

The beauty.

The devotion hidden beneath denial.

Her aura softened, shifting from orange to white—pure, reflective, still.

Some choices were made out of love, even when disguised as distance.

Chapter - 6
The Start

LEE

Saturday, January 2 — 1:00 A.M.

The silence that followed her last words pressed heavily against Lee's chest.

The night had grown colder.

A thin mist drifted across the open space, clinging low to the ground. Fireworks had long faded, leaving behind only smoke and the occasional echo of distant celebration. The city had begun to sleep.

Lee looked at Akshara.

She stood only a few steps away, glowing faintly—no longer a memory shaped by guilt, no longer a voice buried in regret. She was real. Present. Unavoidable.

"Why are you here?" he finally asked.

His voice was calm, controlled—but inside, his thoughts collided chaotically. Why now?

Akshara met his gaze steadily. "I'm here to investigate my death," she said. "To understand the conspiracy behind how I was killed."

The word killed echoed between them, heavier than the night itself.

For a moment, Lee said nothing.

Then she hesitated, something fragile surfacing in her expression. The soft white glow around her dimmed, shifting back toward uncertain blue—like moonlight over water.

"But finding the truth feels impossible," she admitted.

Lee shook his head immediately.

"Nothing is impossible," he said firmly. "Not anymore."

Resolve formed where grief once lived. The same focus that guided his hands in surgery, that carried him through failures and long nights, surfaced now with clarity.

"We'll start," he said. "Somewhere."

Akshara studied him. "Where?"

"The last place you remember clearly," he replied. "That's always the beginning."

"Zee Pub. Hyderabad," she said without hesitation. "That's the last clear memory I have."

"Then that's where we go."

The drive through the city felt unreal.

Hyderabad slept uneasily. Traffic lights blinked over empty roads. Stray dogs moved quietly along sidewalks. Somewhere, music drifted faintly from a distant apartment while shadows clung stubbornly to closed shops.

Zee Pub greeted them with silence.

Boarded windows. Rusted shutters. Faded notices peeling from walls.

“It’s closed,” Lee said quietly. “Illegal activities. The case shut it down years ago.”

“There’s nothing here anymore,” she whispered.

“Then we start with people,” Lee replied. “Your parents. Friends. Anyone who might remember details.”

“It’s too late tonight,” she said.

“Then tomorrow morning.”

Back at his apartment, the air smelled faintly of antiseptic and winter. Lee loosened his collar, jacket falling over a chair. The lights were dim.

Akshara noticed the emptiness immediately.

No photographs. No memories.

“You’re single.”

“Yes.”

“Why aren’t you married?”

“I’m not interested in love.”

The lie came too quickly.

When she spoke of being caught by an Aghori student, understanding settled heavily.

Whatever brought her back—it was not choice.

It was survival.

Outside, winter wind brushed the windows.

Inside, the past—patient, ruthless, and unfinished—had finally returned.

Chapter - 7
No Trace

AVANEESH

Saturday, January 2 — 9:00 A.M.

Avaneesh did not waste time.

The morning air was still cool, winter clinging stubbornly to Hyderabad even as the sun climbed higher. He stood near the window when Lee's call came—sharp, urgent, unmistakable. Avaneesh answered on the first ring.

Before Lee had finished speaking, Avaneesh was already moving.

Formalities could wait. Urgency could not.

He pulled on a dark jacket over his shirt, keys already in his hand, and stepped out into the muted morning traffic. As he drove, he dialed a number he had not used in years—one that still carried weight within the system.

Subash.

An IAS officer.

And an old acquaintance.

Subash listened quietly as Avaneesh explained the situation. No interruptions. No questions. When Avaneesh finished, there was a pause on the line—long enough to feel deliberate, heavy with implication.

"I'll give you a number," Subash finally said. "He's been there for twelve years. Fifty-four years old. Works as an old SI. If anyone knows what was buried in the past, it's him."

The name followed.

Dinesh.

Avaneesh dialed immediately.

No response.

He tried again.

Still nothing.

That silence unsettled him more than an outright refusal ever could.

By the time the sun climbed higher, Avaneesh made a decision Lee had never once asked him to make.

He would go himself.

Lee never asked for help lightly. If he had reached out now, something was deeply wrong.

The Police Station

The police station sat beneath a faded signboard, its paint peeling like neglected memory. The building smelled of dust, damp walls, and aging paper. Ceiling fans rotated lazily, pushing warm air that carried no comfort.

Avaneesh spotted Dinesh immediately.

The man sat at a cluttered desk buried beneath stacks of files, his khaki uniform slightly loose on his frame, sleeves creased from years of habit. His hair was thinning, eyes tired, posture rigid—the dull weight of routine etched permanently into his face.

Avaneesh did not bother with pleasantries.

“Why didn’t you answer my call?” he asked sharply. “I was sent by an IAS officer.”

Dinesh froze.

Color drained from his face. His hands trembled as he stood up abruptly, chair scraping loudly against the floor.

“I—I’m sorry, sir,” he stammered. “I didn’t realize.”

“What’s the purpose of your visit?” Dinesh asked, forcing his voice into something resembling composure.

Avaneesh leaned forward slightly, resting his palms on the desk. “A girl named Akshara,” he said evenly. “She died near the park my friend owns. A few years ago.”

Silence fell.

Not the ordinary kind.

Dinesh’s jaw tightened. His eyes flickered away, avoiding Avaneesh’s gaze. Outside, a police jeep passed, its engine humming indifferently.

“That area,” Dinesh said slowly, carefully, “used to be forest. Before the park was built.”

Then, abruptly, he stood. “I’ll check the records.”

He disappeared into the records room.

Minutes passed.

When Dinesh returned, he carried a thick stack of old files. One by one, he flipped through them, movements mechanical, practiced—too practiced. Papers rustled. Stamps thudded. Files closed again.

Nothing.

No Akshara.

No matching report.

Avaneesh felt something tighten in his chest.

“Check again,” he said firmly. “One month before and one month after January 1, 2018.”

Dinesh nodded and searched again.

Still nothing.

The absence screamed louder than any confession.

Avaneesh stepped aside and called Lee.

“There’s no record,” he said quietly. “Nothing before. Nothing after.”

A pause followed on the other end.

“Okay,” Lee replied calmly. “I’ll call you back in five minutes.”

The line went dead.

Avaneesh walked out of the station, winter sunlight striking his face. Disappointment weighed heavily on him. But as he reached his car, something stopped him.

Dinesh’s face.

The man hadn’t looked relieved.

He had looked afraid.

Avaneesh turned back casually. “Don’t worry,” he said lightly. “I won’t complain to my friend. You’re safe.”

Dinesh swallowed hard and nodded.

But Avaneesh already knew.

Records don’t vanish on their own.

Someone had erased Akshara.

And whoever did it—

Was still afraid.

Chapter - 8
The Shock

AKSHARA

Saturday, January 2 — 7:00 A.M.

Morning arrived, but it meant nothing to me.

The sky lightened slowly, pale winter sunlight spreading across the city. Birds returned hesitantly to electric wires. Shops lifted shutters halfway. Life resumed.

I did not sleep.

Sleep was no longer required for what I had become.

Lee woke late—around seven. By then, I had already been standing by the window, watching Hyderabad reshape itself beneath early light, trying to recognize a city that no longer remembered me.

The air was cool, faintly dusty. The city felt faster now. Sharper.

We had to travel to the other side of town.

I guided him, though it took longer than it should have. Roads had shifted. Familiar landmarks were gone. Buildings rose where empty spaces once breathed. Time had rewritten the map, and the city I knew now existed only inside me.

When we reached my old house, something inside me fractured.

The moment I stepped closer, my aura shifted—from white to copper.

Children were playing outside.

Their laughter froze me in place.

I had never seen them before.

“Lee,” I said quietly, disbelief tightening my voice. “Ask them… what happened here. These aren’t the old tenants.”

Lee spoke to the adults nearby. They wore simple clothes, sweaters pulled tight against the winter air, faces cautious around strangers.

The answer destroyed what little steadiness I had left.

After my body was found—after the death of their only daughter—my mother survived just one month.

Grief consumed her.

She died quietly.

Without justice.

Without answers.

The copper glow around me darkened, sinking into deep blue. Only Lee could see it.

Then anger took over.

Blue ignited into burning red.

“Find the truth,” I demanded, rage tearing through my voice. “I want everything about my case. Now.”

Lee hesitated.

Even he was afraid of what he saw in me.

He began calling people—anyone. No answers. No responses. Only silence.

I screamed.

The sound ripped through the air—violent, raw—but only Lee could hear it. To the tenants, he must have looked insane: standing frozen, eyes wide, reacting to nothing.

They hurried their children inside.

As they did, one small child turned back.

“Bye,” the child said softly.

Not to Lee.

To me.

My anger collapsed instantly.

Red drained away.

Color faded until almost nothing remained.

And I remembered Putri’s words:

Anger destroys clues.

Chapter - 9
A Break

LEE

Saturday, January 2 — 1:00 P.M.
The call came without warning.

My phone vibrated sharply in my hand—once, urgent, unmistakable. For a moment, I considered ignoring it. The investigation had already fractured the morning, and I needed distance from everything that demanded something of me.

Then I saw the name on the screen.

Amma.

The world narrowed instantly.

I answered without speaking. On the other end, her breathing reached me first—uneven, shallow, each inhale sounding borrowed, as though her body had begun negotiating with time.

"Lee…" she said.

Her voice was weak. Fractured. Nothing like the woman who had raised me with quiet authority, who once moved through illness and exhaustion without complaint. This voice trembled, slipping between strength and surrender.

She was ill.

The doctors had not said the word yet, but I heard it in the spaces between her breaths. In the way she paused before sentences, conserving energy. In the way she asked—not ordered—to see me.

"I want you here," she said softly.

For a long moment, I said nothing.

The room around me felt distant. Akshara stood a few steps away, watching—not intruding, not questioning. She did not need to hear the words. The change in my posture was enough. The way my shoulders tightened. The way my hand lowered slowly, as if the phone had suddenly grown heavier.

"I'll come," I said finally.

When the call ended, silence rushed in.

The city outside continued as if nothing had changed—traffic murmuring faintly, winter wind brushing against windows, distant horns rising and falling like indifferent breath.

Akshara spoke first.

"Let's pause the investigation," she said gently. "Be with your mother for a day or two. We can continue after."

There was no urgency in her voice. No trace of resentment. She did not remind me of time lost, or truth delayed. In that moment, she was not a victim seeking justice.

She was simply… understanding.

I nodded.

Some truths could wait.

Some deaths—even unresolved—bowed before the living.

The Road

We left Hyderabad as the afternoon faded.

The city peeled away gradually—traffic thinning, buildings shrinking into silhouettes, glass towers replaced by long stretches of road and dry land. The winter sun dipped low, staining the horizon with pale gold and muted orange before surrendering to dusk.

I drove in silence.

The farther we moved from the city, the quieter the world became. Even my thoughts seemed to echo, stripped of urgency, weighed down by memory. Fields stretched on either side of the road, dry grass whispering softly as wind moved through it. Occasional trees stood alone against the darkening sky, patient and unmoved.

Akshara sat beside me, her presence steady, subdued. Her glow was faint now—neither white nor blue, but something softer, restrained. She watched the road ahead, not the city behind.

By the time darkness settled fully, the palace emerged.

The Palace

It rose from the land like something ancient and watchful.

Stone walls soaked in years of silence. Arched windows darkened by time. Corridors layered with memory rather than decoration. The bog palace did not announce wealth. It endured it.

It was mine.

As we stepped inside, the air shifted—cooler, denser. The faint scent of antiseptic mixed with old stone and winter dampness. Doctors moved with restrained urgency, their footsteps careful, voices lowered out of respect—or caution. Machines hummed softly, their steady rhythm cutting through the stillness.

Akshara studied the space quietly.

“You’re this wealthy,” she said softly, “yet you choose to live simply.”

I said nothing.

Some lives were built for visibility.

Mine was not.

My mother’s condition worsened as night fell.

I changed into simple clothes—dark trousers, a plain shirt—she had never liked extravagance, especially near sickness. The room she lay in was dim, curtains half-drawn, lamps casting warm pools of light against cold stone walls.

Machines whispered around her.

Every sound felt amplified. Every breath felt counted.

Before entering her room, I turned to Akshara.

“One condition,” I said, my tone firm but not unkind. “Do not enter my personal room.”

She did not ask why.

She simply nodded. “I won’t.”

That trust—unquestioned, immediate—settled something inside me.

I went in.

Night

Hours blurred.

Time lost its edges.

I sat beside my mother, measuring recovery not in hours, but in breaths. Occasionally, she opened her eyes and smiled faintly, as though reassuring me rather than herself. I spoke little. Words felt unnecessary.

Eventually, exhaustion overcame vigilance.

Sleep claimed me against my will.

Akshara did not sleep.

Sleep belonged to the living.

For her, time had lost its shape.

As the palace grew unnaturally quiet, boredom did not arrive as restlessness, but as awareness. Endless corridors stretched before her, lamps glowing faintly, shadows clinging stubbornly to corners. The palace breathed slowly, like something alive but reserved.

She wandered.

Not with intent to disobey.

Not with purpose.

Just movement—an echo of being alive.

That was when she crossed the threshold into my room.

The air inside felt different.

Denser.

Heavier.

I lay asleep, unaware.

She turned to leave—

And then she saw it.

The painting.

Completely black.

Not darkness born of absence, but something deeper. A void painted onto canvas. It swallowed light rather than reflected it. Even her presence felt muted near it, as if she were unwelcome.

Something behind it felt wrong.

Contained.

Bound.

Her instincts screamed.

Truth does not hide in darkness—it waits for light.

Her hand lifted slowly toward the switch.

Just one touch.

Just one moment—

A dog barked.

Sharp. Violent. Too sudden.

The sound shattered the stillness like glass.

I woke instantly.

My eyes found her.

Anger surged before thought.

"I told you not to enter this room," I said, my voice colder than the stone walls.

Akshara froze.

She stepped back immediately.

The switch was never turned on.

The painting remained black.

And whatever truth lay behind it remained sealed.

After

Some secrets survive not because they are powerful—

But because the moment to reveal them is always interrupted.

We stayed at the palace for two days.

Time moved differently there.

Mornings arrived quietly. Corridors echoed endlessly. Conversations were brief, careful, restrained. Akshara kept her distance—not out of fear, but respect. She watched over me silently as I stayed by my mother's side.

By the end of the second day, her condition stabilized.

The palace exhaled.

On the morning of January 4, I stood by the window, watching the last traces of night dissolve into pale winter light. The sky felt lighter.

So did the silence.

Akshara appeared beside me.

Her presence was calm—but resolved.

“It’s time,” she said softly.

I nodded.

The pause had ended.

Whatever truth had been buried—by people, by power, by fear—

We were about to dig it up.

Chapter - 10
The Clue

AKSHARA

Saturday, January 3

The call came on **January 3**.

Winter sunlight filtered weakly through the palace windows, pale and uncertain, as though the day itself had not yet decided what it would become. Outside, the grounds were quiet—no birds, no movement—just cold air resting against stone walls.

Avaneesh did not waste time.

When his voice reached Lee, it was low and measured—careful in a way that did not signal caution, but danger.

“The Sub-Inspector of that area,” he said, “Dinesh. Something about him is wrong. Too many gaps. Too many things missing.”

I felt it instantly.

A tightening in the air.

A subtle shift inside my presence.

Lee did not pause to think. He stood up immediately, already reaching for his keys, instinct taking control before reason could catch up. His movements were sharp, decisive—the same way they were before entering an operation theater.

But I stopped him.

"Not today."

He turned toward me, startled. "Why not?"

I met his gaze steadily. My glow remained calm, controlled—soft blue at the edges, steady at the center.

"Your mother is still unwell," I said. "And I know what it feels like—to lose a mother. Or to live with the fear that you might."

The words were quiet, but they carried weight. The truth in them did not need force.

"Pain clouds judgment," I continued. "If we go now, anger will lead us instead of clarity. Let us go tomorrow."

For a long moment, Lee stood frozen between urgency and restraint.

The palace corridor felt colder. Somewhere in the distance, a machine hummed steadily, measuring life in numbers that could change at any moment.

Then, slowly, he nodded.

They would wait.

***

That night, Lee remained alone in his room.

The palace was unusually silent—no footsteps, no distant voices, only the low, constant hum from the medical wing where his mother slept. Outside, wind brushed softly against old stone, carrying the chill of January deeper into the halls.

He sat at his desk beneath a single lamp.

Writing.

Carefully.

Methodically.

The pen moved steadily, as if the words were not being created but released—thoughts that had waited years for permission to exist. Pages filled quietly, one after another, with things that could not yet be spoken aloud.

I entered without sound.

The moment Lee sensed my presence, he closed the diary and slid it aside—too quickly. Too deliberately.

I noticed.

There was something in those pages.

Something unfinished.

Something unresolved.

Something he did not want me to see.

I did not ask.

Some truths require patience more than questions.

As the night deepened, Lee finally spoke.

“There is no official record of you ever being reported missing,” he said, his voice steady but heavy. “No complaint. No identification. Nothing.”

The words settled inside me slowly, like cold rain seeping through skin.

“I confirmed something else,” he continued. “Your body was found near that area—but no one officially identified it as you.”

He paused.

“The place where your body truly was… it was disturbed. Broken out. As if someone tried to erase the scene itself.”

My glow dimmed slightly.

"And Kiran?" I asked quietly.

Lee shook his head. "If Kiran had reported you missing or dead, there would be something. A form. A statement. A witness. Anything."

His jaw tightened.

"But there is nothing."

Silence filled the room.

Heavy.

Suffocating.

Lee leaned back in his chair, staring at the ceiling, as though the answers might be written there.

"All of this leads to one person," he said.

I already knew the name.

"Dinesh," he confirmed. "Only someone in authority could manipulate records this thoroughly. Only someone who controlled that jurisdiction."

My aura shifted.

White drained into a faint, cold blue.

This was no longer about lost memory.

Tomorrow would not be about searching.

Tomorrow would be about truth.

And someone had gone to extraordinary lengths to bury it.

Chapter - 11
The One

LEE

Saturday, January 4 — 7:00 A.M.

January 4 began quietly.

The kind of quiet that feels temporary.

Pale winter light filtered through tall windows of the palace, diffused by thin curtains that softened the morning without warming it. The air was cold but clean, carrying the faint scent of medicine and old stone. Somewhere in the distance, a monitor beeped steadily—slow, patient, alive.

I stood beside my mother's bed.

She looked smaller than I remembered. Fragile. Her skin was pale against white sheets, her breath shallow but steady. When she opened her eyes and saw me, she smiled faintly—an expression that carried trust without question.

“I’ll be away today,” I said softly. “Just for a few hours.”

She nodded gently.

Even now—even weakened—she trusted me without asking why.

That trust felt heavier than any responsibility I had ever carried in hospitals or boardrooms.

Akshara stood a few steps behind me, silent.

Her presence pressed lightly against the room—not heavy, not restless, just *there*. Calm on the surface. Taut underneath. Like water holding back a current.

By the time the sun climbed higher, we were on the road.

***

The Station — Daylight

By afternoon, the police station stood before us again.

In daylight, it looked ordinary. Harmless, even.

Dust-coated walls. A faded emblem above the entrance. Constables moving in and out with routine indifference. Ceiling fans turned lazily, stirring warm air that smelled of paper, sweat, and neglect.

I approached the building the way I approached surgery.

Slowly.

Carefully.

With calculation.

Inside, I spoke to Dinesh.

First directly.

Then indirectly.

I asked questions that sounded casual. I repeated them later with different phrasing. I shifted tone—friendly, professional, distant. I watched his hands. His breath. His eyes.

Nothing changed.

No shaking fingers.

No hesitation.

No mistake.

Every answer he gave was measured, controlled, empty.

Too empty.

When we stepped outside, winter sunlight struck my face—but it did nothing to ease the pressure tightening around my chest.

For the first time that day, control slipped.

Not into panic.

Into helplessness.

Akshara looked at me, her expression unreadable, her glow faint but steady.

“Daylight won’t work,” she said softly.

Her voice was calm. Certain.

“Fear will bring the truth.”

I did not stop her.

***

Night

Night came without ceremony.

By the time Dinesh left the station, the road ahead of him was nearly deserted. Streetlights grew fewer with every kilometer. Darkness thickened, pressing close as trees gathered around the road, their branches forming a canopy that swallowed what little moonlight remained.

His vehicle moved steadily.

Then—

The tire burst.

The sound cracked through the night like a gunshot.

The car swerved violently before scraping to a halt. Gravel scattered across the road. Silence followed—sharp, unnatural.

Both men stepped out.

The constable held a flashlight, its beam cutting weakly through darkness. Dinesh scanned the road, irritation flickering briefly across his face before something colder replaced it.

The air shifted.

Cold spread unnaturally fast—as if the night itself had inhaled and refused to exhale again.

Akshara appeared.

The constable screamed.

The sound was raw. Animal.

His body reacted before his mind could—he turned to run, but I caught him by the collar, gripping hard enough to stop instinct from taking over.

“Stay,” I ordered.

Dinesh didn’t scream.

He ran.

Straight into the forest.

Akshara followed him without hesitation.

***

The Constable

The constable collapsed to the ground, shaking violently. His breath came in broken gasps, eyes darting wildly into darkness behind me.

“Speak,” I said sharply.

He flinched as though the word struck him.

"There were four of them!" he cried. "They met in a red-light area. I don't know their names—I swear. One of them was an SI!"

My stomach tightened.

"He used to bring young girls," the constable continued, voice cracking. "Back when that park was still forest. He had fun with them… then killed them there."

His hands trembled as he wiped his face, tears mixing with dust.

"But none of the bodies were recorded," he whispered. "No reports. No postmortems. Nothing. I don't know how it was possible."

Then his voice dropped again.

"Dinesh's wife found out," he said. "She tried to expose him… and he killed her before she could speak."

The constable broke completely.

I didn't wait.

I ran into the forest.

***

Dinesh

The trees swallowed me immediately.

Branches clawed at my arms. Leaves crushed beneath my shoes. The air was colder here—thick, wrong, suffocating. My breath burned in my chest as I pushed forward, guided only by instinct and the faint disturbances ahead.

And then I saw them.

Akshara had already caught him.

Dinesh was on his knees.

Trapped.

Shaking.

But when he looked up—

His eyes were empty.

Not terrified.

Not remorseful.

Just hollow.

I stepped closer.

"Tell me what you know," I said.

For a moment, I thought he would beg. Lie. Bargain.

Instead, his mouth moved.

"I raped you."

That was all.

No names.

No explanations.

No regret.

The forest itself seemed to stop breathing.

Akshara froze.

And then—

She entered his body.

Before I could shout, his hand moved against his will. His fingers wrapped around his service gun.

The first shot exploded into the trees.

Straight into his chest.

He screamed and collapsed.

Another shot.

Between his knees.

A brutal destruction that trapped him in the dirt—alive, aware, helpless.

Akshara stepped out of him.

She didn't touch him again.

She didn't need to.

Dinesh lay there bleeding, crying, choking on his own suffering. No one came. No help arrived. No mercy followed.

Slowly—

Inevitably—

He died.

***

Aftermath

I reached her moments later.

"There are three more!" I shouted. "Three more people still alive—and now we don't even know their names!"

Her aura burned violently, lighting the forest like living flame.

Then my anger broke.

"You were kind," I said quietly. "Innocent. You trusted people. You smiled easily."

I swallowed hard.

"You weren't made for this darkness."

Akshara looked away.

Her colors flickered—blue, white, orange—unstable, confused, fighting each other.

The ghost she had become struggled against the girl she once was.

We drove back without speaking.

And as I watched her reflection in the windshield, one thought stayed with me—

The hunt was no longer just for the remaining three men.

It was for the part of Akshara

That this world had stolen.

And I didn't know

How much of her innocence would survive

What lay ahead.

Chapter - 12
The Past

AKSHARA

Friday, January 4 — 9:00 P.M.

Memories don't return gently.

They don't arrive like forgotten photographs or harmless dreams. They come like wounds reopening—raw, sudden, and merciless—dragging pain back into places you thought had already healed.

That night, after Dinesh died, something inside me fractured.

It was late—**past nine**. Outside, winter had deepened its hold. The palace lay quiet under a sky without stars, the air heavy with cold and unspoken things. Somewhere far away, wind brushed against stone walls, low and persistent, like fingers testing for weakness.

The colors in my aura wouldn't settle.

They shifted restlessly—blue, white, orange—sometimes slipping into shades I couldn't recognize or name. It felt as though my soul was trying to speak in a language my mind had forgotten. Or refused to remember.

And then it began.

Not in order.

Not cleanly.

Just pieces.

Sharp.

Bleeding.

Unforgiving.

***

I was born into a **middle-class family**—simple, loving, careful.

I was their only child.

Because of that, I was protected more than most. Pampered, even. My parents never said no when it came to things—clothes I liked, books I wanted, school supplies, food, small dreams I didn't yet know how to shape.

But they hesitated when it came to **people**.

The first hurt I remember was not physical.

It happened when I was **eleven**.

Every evening after school, my friends ran outside laughing, their bags tossed aside, uniforms loosened as the sun dipped behind buildings. The air smelled of dust and warmth, of freedom. They played until darkness settled and their mothers called their names from balconies.

I watched from behind gates.

From windows.

From the safe side of permission.

Whenever I asked to join them, my parents always said the same thing.

"We'll come with you."

They believed that was love.

And it *was* love.

But it wasn't the kind a child understands.

Because roaming freely with friends—unwatched, unmeasured—that feeling never belonged to me. Until intermediate, my world was only **home and school**.

Safe.

Silent.

Controlled.

Sometimes, control looks like care.

Sometimes, care becomes a cage without meaning to.

***

Then came **MBBS**.

The college was far from home.

At first, they refused.

Not like strict parents.

Like frightened ones.

Parents who knew the world was not gentle and wanted to keep their only child untouched by it.

They finally agreed only because their friends were faculty there. They believed that way, someone would always be watching. Someone would always be protecting me.

Even from myself.

That was when I met **Kiran**.

He was the first person I spoke to on campus.

Kind.

Gentle.

Smiling in a way that felt safe.

In the beginning, he opened doors, shared notes, spoke softly. He made the college feel less unfamiliar. Less lonely. We became friends naturally.

Too naturally.

So naturally that I didn't notice when he became my comfort.

But comfort doesn't always stay pure.

Slowly, under the influence of his circle, **alcohol** entered his life.

Then cigarettes.

Then late-night fights. Bruised knuckles. Raised voices.

Anger became familiar in him—as if something inside his chest needed violence to breathe.

And still…

I stayed.

Because the girl I was believed **love meant fixing**.

***

Around the same time, **Lee** entered my life too.

Lee was different.

On the surface, he was similar—smart, confident, sharp—but he carried himself with boundaries like walls. He never crossed lines. Never touched what wasn't offered. Never took more than what was given.

And he never showed me his diary.

Not once.

In college, Lee was always present—quietly there, never forcing his presence, yet somehow always near. Always observing. Always aware.

Later, I learned something about him.

Behind closed doors, alone in his room, he drowned himself in alcohol.

One night—late, well past midnight—he called me.

Crying.

At first, I didn't understand why. Later, I realized he meant to call someone else. But by mistake—or weakness—he called me instead.

I heard the pain in his voice.

It wasn't drama.

It was buried. Heavy. Real.

And in that moment, Lee stopped feeling like a rich, untouchable man.

He felt human.

Broken.

***

Then **Kiran proposed**.

He was the only one I spoke to without hesitation. Without fear of judgment. I believed I could change him. Make him softer. Kinder.

Lee didn't know we were in a relationship.

But he heard everything.

He heard me asking Kiran to stop drinking. To stop smoking. To control his anger. To be gentle.

Lee overheard it all.

A few days later, **Lee proposed** to me.

I said no.

I told him the truth—that I was already in a relationship. I said we could still be friends.

Lee looked at me for a long time and said quietly,

"I can't pretend to be your friend once I love you."

After that, something changed.

Not loudly.

Not dramatically.

Distance replaced closeness.

Silence replaced comfort.

And I didn't know then…

that my rejection would be one of the **last normal things** in my life.

***

One day, **Kiran invited me to a party**.

I didn't know how to tell my parents.

Then the New Year festival arrived at college, and I used it as an excuse.

That night, the air was cool and festive. Lights were strung across the campus. Music drifted through open spaces. Laughter echoed.

I **jumped over the wall**.

I went to the party.

At first, everything was fine—music, familiar faces, bright lights that made me feel brave.

Then alcohol entered my body.

My vision dulled.

My head grew heavy.

The world slowed unnaturally.

I asked Kiran to take me home.

He dropped me near my **house gate**.

The street was quiet. Cold. Dimly lit.

That is the last thing I remember clearly.

The gate.

After that—

Something happened.

And that missing moment…

is where my death was born.

Chapter - 13
Extending Clue

LEE

Friday, January 4 — 10:00 P.M.

Before leaving the forest road, I turned back to the constable one last time.

The night had settled completely now. Cold crept up from the ground, seeping through shoes and skin alike. Wind moved unevenly through the trees, carrying the smell of damp earth and crushed leaves. Somewhere far away, the city hummed—indifferent, unaware.

“You will say this if anyone asks,” I said calmly.

“You were with Dinesh until late night. He stopped on that route and made a girl get down. They went inside together. You left from there. It was common for him to bring girls. It was dark, so you couldn’t see her clearly.”

The constable nodded repeatedly.

Fear had erased everything else—authority, pride, curiosity. Survival had reduced him to agreement.

I walked away.

Akshara followed in silence.

For several minutes, the road swallowed our footsteps. Trees leaned inward from both sides, their branches scraping softly, whispering secrets that had lived here too long. Even the distant glow of Hyderabad felt reluctant, as though the city itself refused to claim this place.

After a while, I spoke.

“The constable said something else,” I said quietly.

“He said Dinesh went with a girl that same night. Told him to leave. Said he’d come back.”

I paused.

“He never did.”

Akshara stopped walking.

The air around her thickened—not violently, not loudly—just heavy. Like a storm waiting behind still clouds.

She didn’t need explanation.

It wasn’t one crime.

It was a habit.

***

We reached a road I had hoped I would never bring her to.

Broken streetlights flickered overhead, their yellow glow uneven and tired. Women stood beneath them—leaning against cracked walls, resting on one leg, shifting weight with the kind of patience learned through repetition.

Their dresses told stories before their mouths did.

One wore a tight red dress with a deep neckline—faded just enough to show it had seen too many nights. Another had on a short denim skirt and a loose top that slipped off one shoulder deliberately, as if gravity itself had been trained. A third wore a long black dress with a slit that moved when she walked—slow, practiced, intentional.

Makeup was heavy. Lipstick bold. Perfume strong enough to replace conversation.

Cars slowed.

Windows slid down.

Eyes met briefly—never long enough to feel human.

Lives entered vehicles and disappeared again.

Akshara stopped.

"So many…" she whispered, disbelief cracking her voice.

"How many girls are trapped in this?"

She turned toward me, hesitating.

"Are you…" she searched my face, "…going to take one?"

For a moment, I didn't answer.

Not because I didn't know what to say.

Because I hated that the question even made sense in this world.

Her aura shifted—white to green—uncertainty mixing with discomfort.

"This is where Dinesh used to come earlier," I said evenly. "Later, he started bringing girls with others. Prostitution houses."

I looked down the road.

"This is where we look."

***

The moment I stepped closer, they noticed.

It always happened quickly.

One girl approached first, smiling easily, confidence worn like jewelry. She placed her hand lightly on my arm—familiar, uninvited, practiced.

Another stepped closer from the side, brushing her fingers against my sleeve as if by accident. Her nails were painted bright pink, chipped at the edges. Someone leaned in close enough that perfume replaced oxygen.

“Handsome,” one murmured.

“New face,” another added, eyes flicking over my suit.

“Looks expensive,” a third said with a soft laugh.

My body stiffened immediately.

I wasn’t afraid.

I was uncomfortable—deeply, visibly uncomfortable.

I could feel Akshara watching.

Then she laughed.

Not softly.

“Oh wow,” she said, amused. Her aura shifted from green to bright yellow.

“Relax, Lee. You look like someone just asked you to donate an organ without anesthesia.”

One girl slid her hand slightly higher on my arm.

Akshara leaned closer to me, whispering with mock seriousness,

“Blink twice if you need rescue.”

I clenched my jaw.

Another girl circled behind me, fingertips brushing my shoulder.

“So quiet,” she teased. “You shy?”

Akshara snorted.

“Shy? No. He’s just calculating how many antiseptics are needed after this.”

I shot her a look.

She grinned wider.

"Also," she added cheerfully, "if you touch him again, he might start explaining hospital hygiene rules."

The girls laughed—light, unbothered laughter.

One finally asked, "So what do you want?"

I took a breath.

"Who is the oldest person managing this place?"

They froze.

Confused glances passed between them.

Then one nodded toward the side.

An older woman sat slightly apart—watching everything, saying nothing. She wasn't dressed provocatively. Simple saree. Sharp eyes. Still posture.

Power doesn't advertise.

It observes.

I walked toward her and showed Dinesh's photo.

She studied it for a long moment, longer than comfort allowed.

Then shook her head.

"No."

Akshara leaned in again.

"Oof. Rejected by a criminal *and* his HR department."

I ignored her.

"Which batch?" the woman asked.

"2017."

She nodded slowly.

"Only three from that time are still active."

My pulse quickened.

"One here. Two elsewhere."

She gave me an address.

Then waved dismissively.

“It’s late. Come tomorrow. After five.”

***

As we walked back, Akshara’s yellow glow lingered, playful.

“Well,” she said, satisfied, “that went better than expected. You didn’t faint. Progress.”

“At least you enjoyed it,” I muttered.

“Oh absolutely,” she replied.

“Watching you panic over harmless hands is the best entertainment I’ve had since I died.”

She laughed again—open, unrestrained.

And for a brief moment…

she didn’t feel like a ghost.

She felt like **Akshara**.

***

Later that night, my phone rang.

One of my junior doctors.

“Sir, will you be available tomorrow?”

“Yes,” I said. “I’ll come.”

Until evening, we had nothing else to do.

But somewhere in Hyderabad’s endless noise, light, and shadow—

Three names were still waiting.

And we were getting closer.

Chapter - 14
The Junior

AKSHARA

Saturday, January 5 — 10:00 A.M.

Morning arrived softly.

Winter sunlight filtered through the hospital's glass façade, pale and restrained, like it knew this was not a place for warmth—only clarity. Outside, Hyderabad moved with its usual impatience: vendors arguing with customers, buses coughing black smoke, horns punctuating the air like accusations.

Inside the hospital, the world obeyed different laws.

Controlled.

Measured.

Alive.

Lee walked ahead of me through the automatic doors. His pace was steady, familiar—long strides, shoulders squared, mind already elsewhere. I followed, not as a body but as presence. A shadow without weight. A thought that refused to leave.

I stayed close.

Not because I needed protection.

Because he had become my only anchor to the living.

The hospital smelled of antiseptic, faint detergent, and coffee that had been reheated too many times. Nurses crossed corridors with quiet urgency, files tucked under their arms, stethoscopes swinging like pendulums measuring borrowed time. Somewhere, a trolley rattled past, metal wheels echoing against polished floors.

Even in winter, the air inside was warm—regulated, obedient, predictable.

We stopped near the cafeteria.

That was when she appeared.

Alena.

She didn't announce herself. She didn't command attention. And yet, attention moved toward her naturally, the way water flows toward a dip in the ground.

She was Lee's junior.

From his college days.

I understood it instantly—not from words, but from posture. From familiarity that did not ask permission. From the way she stood beside him without hesitation, as if she had once learned where he belonged in a room.

Back then, Lee had been invisible in a different way. He moved through college with tunnel vision—buried in schedules, lectures, discipline. He lived like someone already late for a future no one else could see.

He didn't linger.

Didn't socialize.

Didn't notice people unless they interrupted his trajectory.

Girls like Alena—quiet, observant, patient—were never in his line of sight.

Her white coat rested perfectly on her shoulders—clean, crisp, authoritative. When she slipped it off, I noticed her dress beneath: long, pink, lightly floral. Simple. Feminine. Elegant without effort. A thin silver chain rested at her collarbone. Small earrings caught the light each time she turned her head.

Her hair—dark, thick, long—fell freely down her back in soft waves. Not styled to impress. Just… there. Like beauty that didn't know it needed to defend itself.

Her smile reached Lee first.

"Lee," she said warmly. "What happened? Are you okay? Health-wise… financially… anything?"

The concern in her voice wasn't professional.

It wasn't curiosity.

It was care.

Something inside me shifted before I could stop it. My aura softened, warming into a faint pink glow—the color of something I remembered but could no longer touch.

Lee replied calmly. Almost coldly.

"I'm here to clarify your doubts," he said. "Let's go point by point."

She didn't flinch. Didn't look offended. She simply nodded, as if she had learned long ago that warmth was not something she would receive easily from him.

She handed him the report.

That's when I noticed her hands.

Fresh mehndi—dark, detailed, curling across her fingers and palms like someone had written patience onto her skin. The patterns were careful. Intentional. Someone had taken time.

Someone had cared.

And suddenly—I felt irritated.

Not loudly.

Not dramatically.

Just a quiet, sharp discomfort.

The way Lee spoke to her.

The way he failed to see what she was offering without asking.

Alena explained the medical details, voice clear, confident. But her eyes betrayed her. They drifted back to Lee again and again—not searching, not pleading.

Just hoping.

She wasn't just talking.

She was looking.

That's when I understood.

She loved him.

Not recklessly.

Not suddenly.

This had grown quietly—from college days, from watching him from the back rows, from noticing what he never realized was noticed.

And Lee?

He stayed buried in the report—clinical, precise, detached—as if emotions were unnecessary variables in a life he had already optimized.

Something twisted inside me.

Not jealousy.

Frustration.

When she finished and turned to leave, I stopped her.

"Wait," I said gently.

She turned back, surprised.

"Is there something special today?" I asked.

Her smile softened, almost shy. "It's my birthday."

Lee responded instantly.

"Happy birthday."

And stopped.

She stood there.

Not begging.

Not expecting miracles.

Just… waiting.

That was it.

I snapped.

"ASK HER IF SHE'S FREE TILL FOUR."

Lee flinched.

Actually flinched.

He glanced around instinctively, then looked at her—awkward now. "Are you free till four?"

Her face lit up instantly, as if she had been holding happiness behind her ribs and it had finally found a way out.

"Yes."

"ASK HER FOR A PARTY."

He hesitated.

I didn't give him time.

"Do you want to go out?" he asked finally. "We can… celebrate."

"Yes," she said quickly, almost afraid he'd take it back. "I even wanted to go."

"When will we start?" Lee asked.

"Five minutes," she replied—and ran.

Through the half-open door, I heard her laugh with her friends.

"Sorry, I can't give a party today. My family is calling."

Gentle teasing followed.

"No problem, we'll celebrate tomorrow."

She returned, trying—and failing—to hide her excitement.

***

The Mall

At the mall entrance, I told her, "Wait here. Five minutes."

Then I turned to Lee.

"Dress well."

He blinked. "Why?"

"Because," I said firmly, "for once, don't look like someone attending a funeral."

He sighed—but obeyed.

The moment he entered the store, the atmosphere changed.

Staff straightened. Managers appeared. Voices dropped.

This wasn't fear.

It was recognition.

This is his mall.

The realization settled into me completely.

Lee wasn't just wealthy.

He was the kind of wealthy that bent space quietly.

I chose a light blue suit—soft pastel, clean, calm. A white shirt beneath.

"Change."

He obeyed.

When he stepped out, even I paused.

The suit fit him like it had been waiting—broad shoulders, composed posture, quiet authority.

Not loud.

Not arrogant.

Unreal.

When we returned, Alena froze.

Her eyes widened.

For a second, she forgot how to breathe.

***

The Drop

The drive home was quieter. Traffic thinned. Streetlights blurred into gentle streaks.

Alena spoke softly.

"If you hadn't come today…" she hesitated. "I really love you."

Lee stopped the car.

Silence filled the space.

Not awkward.

Heavy.

He didn't turn to her immediately.

"I don't deserve that," he said quietly.

She smiled sadly. "You don't get to decide what I feel."

He finally looked at her.

"You're my junior," he said gently. "And back then… I didn't even notice you. Not because you weren't there—but because I wasn't really living."

She listened without interruption.

“You’re here to study,” he continued. “You have a future that shouldn’t orbit around someone like me.”

Her eyes shimmered.

“I don’t want you to save me,” she whispered. “I just wanted you to notice me.”

That hit him harder than her confession.

Lee swallowed.

“I noticed,” he said. “That’s why I’m stopping this.”

Her smile stayed.

But tears filled her eyes.

“Yeah,” she whispered. “I forgot.”

She stepped out.

Smiling.

Crying.

And I stood beside him, watching her walk away.

Confused.

Because for the first time—

I couldn’t tell if Lee was protecting her.

Or punishing himself.

Chapter - 15
The Prisoners

LEE

Saturday, January 5 — 4:10 P.M.

The sun was already lowering when we reached the distant red-light area.

Winter evening crept in quietly, like it didn't want to be blamed for what it illuminated. Neon boards flickered awake one by one, washing broken walls in artificial color. Music leaked from somewhere—too loud, too cheerful—while the sky dimmed into bruised shades of orange and grey.

The city pretended to celebrate.

It always did.

The moment I stepped out of the car—

Hands.

Eyes.

Voices.

My suit only made it worse.

The women noticed instantly. Some leaned forward, others straightened up, adjusting straps, smoothing skirts, pulling jackets slightly open. Clothing here wasn't fashion—it was negotiation.

One girl wore a short silver dress that reflected the neon lights like broken glass. Another had a tight green top and faded jeans, heels worn thin from standing too long. Someone else wrapped a shawl loosely around a sleeveless black dress, the fabric slipping down every time she moved, as if even cloth was tired of holding on.

Fingers brushed my sleeve.

Not desperate.

Not seductive.

Automatic.

Akshara chuckled beside me.

"Congratulations," she said lightly. "You've officially entered the 'uncomfortable rich man' category."

I stiffened.

Another girl leaned closer, tilting her head. "You look serious," she said. "First time?"

Akshara leaned toward me, whispering,

"Relax. If you panic any harder, they'll start charging you extra for emotional damage."

I ignored her.

By the third place, my chest felt tight—not fear, not disgust.

Dread.

What if there were no clues left?

What if every door led only to silence?

Then—

"I know him."

The voice came from behind the counter.

A girl stepped forward.

She wasn't loud.

She wasn't trying to attract anyone.

She wore a simple black dress—knee-length, plain, practical. No glitter. No performance. Her hair was tied back, not styled. Faint marks lingered near her neck, half-hidden by makeup that had learned its job too early.

She looked young.

Too young.

"How?" I asked.

"He was my first customer," she replied calmly.

The words didn't shock.

They *crushed.*

"When did you start?" I asked.

"Seven years ago."

I forced myself to breathe.

"How old are you now?"

"Twenty-one."

Behind me, Akshara's voice dropped—no humor left.

"Ask why."

I didn't want to.

I did anyway.

"Why… so young?"

The girl didn’t look away.

“My father died because of alcohol when I was twelve,” she said. “My mother managed somehow. Then she discovered my father had an affair. When people found out… society decided she was dirty.”

She paused, eyes unfocused.

“No relatives wanted me. They said a girl from that house would ‘ruin’ theirs.”

Her lips curved—not into a smile.

Into understanding.

“I went to a police station. Dinesh was the in-charge.”

My fists clenched.

“He said he’d help,” she continued. “He placed me here. Younger girls earned him more.”

She looked at the ground.

“Before that… he kept me with him for two days.”

Akshara’s aura burned deep red—contained, lethal.

I had avoided looking at her.

Avoided this place.

Avoided these stories.

Avoided seeing what wealth and distance had protected me from.

Now I couldn’t escape.

“Society likes labels,” the girl added quietly.

“Once they call you ‘characterless,’ everything done to you becomes justified.”

Akshara stepped closer, her voice steady but sharp.

“Men rape and are called victims of temptation.

Women survive and are called shame.”

The girl nodded once.

"At least I'm alive," she said. "Some girls aren't. Some bodies are found, but no one comes to identify them. And if no one names you… you never existed."

My throat burned.

"How many others?" I asked.

"Only two more," she said. "Not three."

That jolted me.

"You're sure?"

"Yes."

"What do they do now?"

"One is a cab driver."

"And the other?"

She hesitated. Then—

"A doctor."

My stomach dropped.

"Where?"

"A hospital that was seized for organ trafficking. I don't remember the name."

Everything aligned with horrifying precision.

The erased records.

The missing bodies.

My old hospital.

They hadn't just killed.

They'd *used*.

I stepped aside and made the call.

"One hour," my contact said.

I returned to her.

“What’s your name?” I asked—finally.

“Juicy.”

I nodded. “Stay with us tonight. If you remember anything—anything—it matters.”

She misunderstood immediately.

“Twenty thousand,” she said flatly.

“No,” I replied. “Not like that.”

She studied my face.

Then nodded.

In the car, silence hung thick.

Hyderabad passed outside—bright malls, traffic, laughter spilling onto roads that had never asked questions.

“Is everyone’s story the same?” I asked quietly.

Juicy stared out the window.

“Yes,” she said. “Pull too hard—we break. Let go—we fall.”

I swallowed.

“Some choose this life, right?” I asked.

She smiled—not kindly.

“No. The ones who choose money don’t come here. They sell dreams elsewhere—using love, marriage, respectability.”

I glanced at Akshara.

Her aura had turned green.

Not calm.

Processing.

“Are you okay?” I asked softly.

She didn’t answer.

Juicy turned toward me. “Who are you talking to?”

“No one,” I said.

But I knew—

Akshara wasn’t silent.

She was remembering.

And the more she remembered…

the closer we came to the truth.

The truth that didn’t just kill her—

but tried to erase her existence.

Chapter - 16
The Body

AKSHARA

Saturday, January 5 — 7:30 P.M.

The word *unrecognised* refused to leave me.

It didn't behave like ordinary thoughts—the kind you can push aside, distract yourself from, or let dissolve into silence. This one stayed. It circled endlessly, feeding on itself, like a vulture that had found something dead and decided it could wait forever.

Juicy had said it without emotion. Without hesitation. As if it were just another fact in a world already full of ugly truths.

Some bodies are never recognised.

The sentence sounded harmless on the surface.

Like a statistic.

Like a line printed in small font at the bottom of a newspaper column.

Like something people read, shake their heads at briefly, and forget before turning the page.

But I had recognised mine.

I had seen myself.

And once you see something like that, you don't forget it—not even after death.

The memory did not return gently.

It did not knock.

It broke in.

Not in fragments. Not in merciful pieces.

But whole. Complete. Violent in its clarity.

I saw myself exactly as I had been left.

My body lay twisted at an angle no living body should ever hold. One leg bent beneath me unnaturally, joints strained past their limits, the other stretched forward as if someone had dragged me and then decided I was no longer worth the effort. Blood had pooled where it should never have been—dark, thick, already cooling into the soil beneath me.

My clothes were not just torn.

They were discarded.

Thrown away in different directions, scattered carelessly, as though they had been removed impatiently—angrily—without thought, without pause, without acknowledgment that they belonged to a person. My top lay several feet away, ripped at the shoulder. My skirt was twisted and stretched, fabric ruined, no longer something meant to be worn.

Like I was no longer something meant to be protected.

My skin told the rest of the story.

Bruises layered over bruises.

Fingerprints dark and unmistakable, pressed into arms, thighs, waist—marks that spoke of force, not accident. My hair—once neat, once cared for—was uneven, clutched and pulled out in places, strands scattered across the ground like evidence no one bothered to collect.

My face hurt to look at.

Lips split.

Swollen.

Discolored.

As if even my mouth had been punished for existing.

I did not look like a girl.

I did not look like a human being.

I looked like something that had been *used.*

And then—

The stick.

It lay beside me, half-hidden in grass, smeared dark with blood. Not broken. Not accidental. Placed there deliberately, like a final insult left behind for the world to see.

I could not remember the moment itself. My mind refused to replay it. But my body remembered what my memory would not allow.

Not as images.

As sensation.

Like a wound remembering the blade.

Like skin remembering hands that never asked permission.

One side of my chest had been swollen unnaturally—distorted, wrong, painful even to imagine. The shape of it told a story my mind did not want to complete. Even now, even as something no longer living, the image of it made my aura darken.

Not because I chose to.

Because I could not stop it.

My anger did not come from ego.

It came from humiliation.

From being reduced to something less than human.

Lee drove beside me, posture straight, hands steady on the steering wheel. His eyes stayed fixed on the road, calm in a way that felt almost cruel.

Too calm.

Too controlled.

I watched him from the corner of my vision and wondered how someone so alive could sit beside someone who had already died once—and keep breathing normally. How his lungs could work when the air inside me felt poisonous.

Streetlights passed in steady rhythm, mocking time itself. Cars moved around us—families, couples, strangers—ordinary lives crossing our path without knowing what sat inside this car.

I felt doubt rise quietly.

Sharp.

"Lee," I said softly, "according to the pattern… they should have taken me to the hospital."

He didn't respond.

"To sell the organs," I continued. "That was the plan. That was what they did to others."

My voice dropped.

"But they didn't."

Silence stretched between us.

"They left me there," I said. "Why?"

Lee's grip tightened—just slightly. A movement small enough to miss if you didn't know him.

But I knew him.

That was the Lee who solved impossible cases.

The Lee who did not need emotion to find truth.

His mind was already cutting through possibilities like a surgeon through flesh.

Before he could speak—

A dog ran across the road.

Small.

Fast.

Sudden.

Juicy screamed.

“MISS IT!”

Lee swerved instinctively.

The world spun.

Metal struck wood.

Glass rattled violently.

The car shuddered as if it had been punched by something enormous.

Then—

Stillness.

Silence rushed in so fast it felt like drowning.

No screams.

No blood.

No broken bones.

Only breathing.

Juicy’s came in sharp, panicked bursts.

Lee’s was slow, controlled—forced back into obedience.

And mine—

Nothing.

Because I did not breathe.

That realization felt colder than the accident itself.

Juicy's fingers clenched into the seat, knuckles drained white. She looked at Lee—then at the empty passenger seat beside him—then back at Lee again.

Her eyes narrowed.

Confusion gave way to unease.

Lee stayed still longer than necessary, as if commanding his heart to behave.

Then his phone vibrated.

The PDF.

The report.

He opened it slowly, scrolling once. Twice. Then turned the screen toward Juicy.

Her face changed instantly.

Not confusion.

Recognition.

"I know him."

Lee's focus sharpened. "Who?"

"Not a doctor," she said. "An ambulance driver."

Lee scrolled again.

Single.

No fixed address.

Temporary numbers.

A man built to disappear.

He made the call.

“Where is he working now?”

A pause.

“Decod Hospital.”

Lee ended the call.

“We’re going there.”

Juicy stared at him.

“You’re… okay, right?” she asked cautiously, eyes flicking again to the empty seat.

Lee nodded, but his gaze shifted slightly toward me.

“Don’t worry,” he said softly—to no one Juicy could see.

She swallowed hard.

***

Inside Decod Hospital, the air smelled like disinfectant and denial. Too white. Too clean. Like a place trying very hard to convince the world it had never done anything wrong.

I found him in the chaos.

Followed him.

Into the mortuary.

When he stood alone with the body, I entered her.

The temperature dropped.

Lights flickered.

He turned.

Saw fear for the first time.

He begged.

Cried.

Promised everything.

I asked.

He answered.

Darshan.

The drug.

The memory loss.

They didn't just kill me.

They tried to erase me.

When I left him shaking, I returned upstairs to find Lee about to enter.

"He's not here," I said.

Lee studied my face—suspicion sharp and painful.

Juicy watched, confused and frightened.

"Who are you talking to?" she whispered.

Lee didn't answer her.

He nodded—to me.

On the drive back, Juicy pressed herself into the seat, silent, eyes darting to the mirror whenever Lee murmured something under his breath.

At home, the report confirmed it.

Darshan.

One of the three.

Then the news flashed.

Ambulance Driver Found Dead in Decod Hospital

Lee turned to me slowly.

"Was that you?"

I didn't answer.

He exploded.

“You are here to investigate,” he shouted, “not to decide who lives and who dies!”

Juicy flinched violently.

She stared at Lee now—not confused anymore.

Afraid.

He was yelling at empty space.

I tried to explain.

He didn’t hear me.

My aura darkened—not rage-black.

Despair-black.

“If you kill again,” Lee said coldly, “I walk away.”

I nodded immediately.

“Okay.”

His eyes were red.

He walked into his room and slammed the door.

The sound echoed like a gunshot.

Juicy whispered, shaking, “Lee… you’re scaring me.”

And in that silence—

I understood something worse than death.

Loneliness.

For the first time since the cave…

I was truly alone.

Chapter - 17
Life of Lee

LEE

Sunday, January 6 — 1:00 A.M.

The door slammed.

The sound cracked through the corridor like a gunshot—sharp, final—then collapsed into a silence so deep it felt as though the house itself had decided to stop breathing.

Lee stood with his back pressed against the door, unmoving, as if the wood behind him could restrain the storm rising in his chest. His breathing was too fast. Not panic.

Something worse.

Something older.

His hands were clenched so tightly that his nails dug into his palms, carving crescents into skin. Veins rose along his wrists—thick, visible, alive. The same way they used to when he was younger, when rage came easily and restraint felt like weakness.

He closed his eyes.

And the first thing he saw was not Akshara.

It was his father.

A politician who never shouted because he never needed to.

Power arrived before him. It entered rooms silently and settled into people's bones. It made grown men stand straighter. Made mothers pull their children closer without knowing why.

Lee remembered a day he never spoke about.

A small house. Ordinary. Cracked walls. A single bulb flickering inside. The smell of cooking oil, dust, and survival. The family living there had opposed his father publicly. Not rebellion.

Opinion.

But in Lee's childhood, opinion was treated like betrayal.

Machines arrived like executioners.

A bulldozer's blade tore into the wall. Concrete cracked. Screams split the air. A woman tried to grab a suitcase and was shoved aside. Children cried. Dust filled lungs and eyes. Panic tasted like metal.

Lee stood beside his father and watched.

Not with horror.

With curiosity.

With the cold fascination of a boy learning what authority could do.

When the house collapsed into rubble, his father didn't blink. He adjusted his cufflinks, calm as if he had corrected a minor inconvenience.

"People are replaceable," his father had said once—like it was a lesson.

And back then, Lee believed him.

He grew up believing consequences were myths invented for the powerless. Money covered everything. Influence erased mistakes. Apologies were for people who couldn't afford silence.

By tenth class, drugs were routine.

Cigarettes were constant.

Alcohol was a companion.

Violence wasn't anger—it was entertainment.

Pain—his or anyone else's—was just background noise.

Hyderabad sharpened the worst parts of him.

He moved to the bed and sat down heavily, shoulders sagging as though his spine was exhausted from carrying him. Then he lay back, staring at the ceiling.

Blank.

Indifferent.

Just like the past he tried to bury.

The junior lecturer came back to him then.

The man had been harmless. Educated. Older. His crime was insisting on discipline—attendance, deadlines, respect. Things Lee considered insults.

The memory tasted bitter now.

The slap had come easily. Too easily. The shock on the man's face—fear mixed with disbelief—had thrilled Lee in a way that disgusted him now.

I enjoyed the fear in his eyes, Lee thought.

And that was the most unforgivable part.

Birthdays followed a ritual carved into excess.

Farmhouse.

Loud music shaking the walls.

Alcohol passed like currency.

Fifteen friends laughing like the world owed them everything.

And girls.

Always girls.

Not invited.

Booked.

They didn't come through streets or chance. They came through numbers saved under coded names. Through online portals disguised as "massage services," "private companionship," "party arrangements." Photographs curated. Prices fixed. Delivery promised.

Human beings reduced to logistics.

Three girls would arrive—told where to sit, how to dress, when to smile. Treated like accessories placed into a room to complete the aesthetic.

Lee remembered sitting apart, glass half full, expression bored.

He told himself he was different because he didn't touch them.

Now he knew the truth.

Not touching didn't make him innocent.

It made him a spectator.

And spectators were not clean.

They were silent participants.

The farmhouse memory slowed—became crueler.

A guy staggered toward him, drunk and laughing.

"One of the three wants sex," he said, grinning.

Lee had been arrogant. Poisoned.

"I'll never touch cheap waste," Lee had replied.

And he meant it.

Not because he respected her.

But because he believed she was beneath him.

That arrogance drove him inside—to beat her, not because she had done wrong, but because his ego wanted a target.

He remembered her running into the washroom.

The click of the door.

Him waiting outside, irritated, tapping fingers against the wall, hatred buzzing without reason.

Then she came out.

And something stopped him.

Nail marks on her chest—thin, red, fresh. Blood still visible. When she turned to close the door, he saw her back.

Lines.

Scratches.

Layered violence written into skin.

She didn't cry dramatically.

She didn't beg.

Her voice was calm—not from strength, but from exhaustion.

"I heard your friends saying you don't touch girls," she said quietly. "I called you because I just need rest. They won't stop. I needed time."

That sentence broke something.

Not because Lee suddenly became good.

But because he finally saw her as a person.

Not a service.

Not a body.

A human being trying not to shatter.

He told her to sleep.

He stood guard—not heroic, just ashamed enough to protect her from men he had been laughing with an hour earlier.

Then the banging started.

Drunk voices.

Jokes.

“Done yet?”

“Destroy her with your strength.”

Their laughter made Lee sick.

And something terrifying surfaced:

If he continued like this—

If he stayed in that circle—

He would become his father.

Not with politics.

With power.

With cruelty.

With entitlement.

The next day, he stopped cocaine.

Stopped cigarettes.

The body rebelled.

Withdrawal was war.

Veins screamed. Skin crawled. Heart raced like prey. Sleep vanished. Food tasted like ash. He punched walls until his knuckles split. Broke mirrors because he couldn’t stand his reflection. Walked rooms like a trapped animal.

He tried dark chocolate.

It was pathetic.

Alcohol stayed—because alcohol didn’t fight back. It softened edges. Made forgetting easier.

Then MBBS began.

And Akshara entered his life.

She didn’t save him.

She didn’t fix him.

She simply existed—disciplined, grounded, unyielding.

She had rules.

Stop drinking.

Stop smoking.

Dress properly.

Respect people.

Lee heard her saying them to Kiran.

And without admitting it—he applied them to himself.

Not for approval.

For survival.

When he proposed, he was terrified.

When she rejected him, he felt pain—not rage.

Then she vanished.

Then she died.

He bought the land.

Built the park.

Planted flowers like apologies.

Ran into success.

Erased his past.

But love didn’t leave.

It just became quiet.

And now—

She was back.

Angry.

Broken.

Unfinished.

Lee turned toward the wall, fists trembling—not with desire to hurt, but with fear of how easily he could.

Violence terrified him now.

Not because he couldn't do it.

Because he could.

And because righteousness made violence feel justified.

He remembered Akshara's look earlier.

Fear.

Restraint.

And that haunted him more than ghosts.

"I won't become him," Lee whispered.

Not his father.

Not his friends.

Not the men who broke her.

But justice without blood demanded patience.

And Lee wasn't sure how much of that he had left.

He was tired.

Existentially.

The kind of tired that comes when the universe hands you back your past and says—

Finish it.

Sleep didn't come.

And in the dark, Lee understood the truth:

Akshara wasn't just his love.

She was his responsibility.

And this time—

Running was not an option.

Chapter - 18
The Third

AKSHARA

Sunday, January 6 — 7:00 A.M.

Fear sat heavy inside me.

Not the fear of death—I had crossed that bridge already and learned how hollow it was.

This fear was sharper.

Colder.

It was Lee's anger.

Because Lee's rage wasn't like mine—wild, burning, reckless.

His rage was disciplined.

Quiet.

Patient.

The kind that didn't explode.

The kind that waited.

The kind that destroyed slowly and cleanly.

When he slammed the door the night before, the sound cut through the house like a warning meant only for me. Even the walls seemed to freeze afterward, as if the furniture itself had learned caution.

I stood outside his room for a long time.

Too long.

My hand lifted once—hesitant—like knocking still meant something in my world. Like apologies still had weight.

I wanted to explain.

I didn't do it for revenge.

I did it because I couldn't watch it happen again.

But I didn't knock.

Because Lee wasn't angry at what I had done.

He was afraid of what I was becoming.

And I didn't want to be the reason he broke.

***

Morning

January 6.

One day left for me.

That truth lived inside me like a ticking clock—not loud, not dramatic, just relentless.

Lee never came out that night.

No pacing.

No water.

No sound.

Only the distant hum of Hyderabad living its ordinary life while mine raced toward its end.

Juicy slept on the sofa, curled into herself, makeup smudged, hair tangled across her face. Her breathing was heavy—the kind of sleep only people with long trauma ever fall into.

I stayed near her.

Not touching.

Because peace—however temporary—should not be disturbed.

As dawn arrived, winter sharpened. The floor tiles felt like stone. The air sliced through gaps in windows. Even the curtains looked stiff, unwilling to move.

Around seven, Juicy began to shiver.

Her lips trembled. Her arms tightened around herself, but it wasn't enough. She looked impossibly small—like someone who had spent her entire life being placed where she didn't belong.

Something softened inside me.

I floated into Lee's room.

Quietly.

Carefully.

Like entering a temple.

He lay facing the wall, blanket half thrown aside.

His face looked wrong.

Not injured.

Not sick.

But broken.

His cheeks were swollen. His eyes red and sunken, skin tight from crying too much and refusing sleep afterward.

Lee had cried.

A lot.

For a moment, I just watched.

There were things I could no longer do.

I couldn't touch his face.

I couldn't hold his hand.

I couldn't sit beside him and lie that everything would be okay.

All I could do was exist.

Like a shadow.

Like memory.

I covered Juicy with a bedsheet. Her shaking eased. She didn't wake.

Then I returned to Lee's bedside and sat there—watching—wishing stupidly that I was still alive.

He woke around ten.

Slowly.

His eyes found me instantly.

He saw me.

But said nothing.

No anger.

No warmth.

No acknowledgment.

That emptiness hurt more than his shouting.

***

Juicy Leaves

Lee woke Juicy gently.

She panicked immediately.

"I was supposed to report by nine," she said, voice shaking. "I need to give money to my executor."

Lee didn't question her.

Didn't judge.

He simply handed her a thick bundle of cash.

"Take this," he said quietly. "And rest for a month."

Juicy froze.

Too much money.

Far more than the world ever believed she deserved.

Her eyes filled. Words failed her.

Lee booked a cab himself. Dropped her personally.

Because he couldn't let another woman walk into danger again.

When he returned, silence followed him.

I stood near the wall, guilt heavy in my chest.

"I'm sorry," I whispered.

Lee paused.

Looked at me once.

"Don't be sorry," he said quietly.

Then—after a pause—

"Be better."

Those words cut deeper than anger.

Because disappointment from Lee felt like losing the only person who had stayed.

***

The Hospital

Lee reopened the report.

Froze.

"Darshan," he murmured. "He worked in my old hospital."

That hospital was gone now—seized, sealed, erased.

This hospital was new.

Bigger.

More floors.

More chaos.

We left immediately.

The building smelled of antiseptic and buried history. A place too clean to be innocent.

Darshan was on leave.

Of course he was.

I saw Alena.

Plain white kurta. No glow. No confidence. Like a flower starved of light.

Her eyes lit briefly when she saw Lee—then dulled again.

Lee remained unreadable.

We asked about Darshan.

She hesitated, then said her friend saw him go downstairs—toward operation theatres.

Lee knew instantly something was wrong.

There were no theatres downstairs.

***

Delay

Security stopped us.

Permissions.

Clearance.

Authority.

Lee waited twenty minutes.

His body remained still—broad shoulders squared, posture controlled, jaw clenched. Every muscle looked restrained, not relaxed. Like a weapon choosing not to fire.

"This isn't normal," he said finally.

He demanded access.

The head was in a meeting.

Lee understood then.

They were buying time.

He went ahead anyway.

I didn't follow immediately.

The hospital was massive.

More floors.

More corridors.

More doors.

By the time I found the right path—

Lee was already inside.

***

The Fight

The checking room was chaos.

Twelve men unconscious.

Some slumped in chairs.

Some against walls.

Some on the floor like discarded weight.

Lee sat in the corner.

Shirt torn.

Blood drying on his knuckles.

Breathing calm—but hollow.

Like something inside him had stepped away and left instinct behind.

His body looked carved from discipline—tension held under control, strength contained rather than released. A man who could destroy—and hated that he could.

On the floor lay Darshan.

Dead.

I stared.

“Did you ask him anything?” I asked.

“No,” Lee said. “They attacked first. There was no time.”

***

Control

When Darshan’s phone rang, Lee answered.

“I’m Lee,” he said calmly.

“Darshan confessed everything on video.”

Pause.

“Call the police and surrender—or it goes public.”

The head panicked.

Police arrived.

Paper trails surfaced.

Approvals.

Transactions.

Organ trafficking.

The head was arrested.

Lee was warned not to leave the city.

***

Leaving

We went to the park.

The place where my life ended.

Lee stood there silently.

He wanted to speak.

Didn't.

I turned away.

And left.

***

Forest

Putri waited.

"You believe your work is done," he said.

"I do," I replied.

Then—

The truth struck.

Why wasn't my body sold immediately?

How did they know Kiran?

Why was the letter sent only to him?

There were four.

Juicy knew only three.

Which meant—

The fourth was close.

Close enough to know me.

Close enough to betray me.

Fear surged.

"He doesn't know," I whispered. "Lee thinks it's over."

Putri stepped aside.

“Then go,” he said.

I turned back toward the city.

Toward Lee.

Toward the final truth.

Before the last jar broke.

Before I became silence.

Before it was too late.

Chapter - 19
The Fourth

LEE

Saturday, January 7 — 3:00 P.M.

I sat on the cold stone bench in the park, staring at the flowers as if they might answer me.

Winter sunlight spilled weakly through the trees—bright enough to show everything, too pale to warm anything. Hyderabad looked stripped of its usual arrogance today, the sky washed thin like someone had rubbed color out of it. Even the wind moved carefully, as though it didn't want to disturb this place.

But nothing here was peaceful.

Not for me.

Not for her.

The park was quiet, but quiet never meant clean.

The flowers in front of me were the same ones I had chosen with deliberate care—marigolds, jasmine, roses she once liked without ever saying she liked them. Some were still alive, standing tall. Others had begun to wilt, petals curling inward like tired fingers giving up.

I planted them with money, guilt, and silence.

This place was never meant to be a park.

It wasn't charity.

It wasn't business.

It was an apology I built because I didn't know how to speak.

A confession made of soil and light because words had failed me when they mattered most.

The wind brushed past again, carrying a faint trace of night jasmine.

My chest tightened.

Not because she wore it.

Not because she owned it.

Because it suited her.

Soft.

Clean.

Quietly unforgettable.

I had seen blood before.

Held lives between my fingers inside operation theatres.

Stared at death without blinking.

But guilt—

Guilt was heavier.

Because criminals could be punished.

Death could be accepted.

But guilt stayed alive.

It ate slowly.

And it never finished.

I should have told her.

That thought came back like a sentence I could never appeal.

I should have told her I loved her before she became memory.

I should have stopped hiding behind pride.

I should have said something when friendship wasn't enough.

The park stayed silent, but my mind was loud.

Her laugh.

Her voice.

Her eyes.

And then the emptiness after she disappeared.

I was so deep inside that noise that I didn't notice the air changing at first.

But my body noticed.

A sudden cold—not winter cold.

Something sharper.

Something wrong.

The hairs on my arms rose.

The jasmine scent vanished.

The leaves above trembled though the wind stopped completely.

Then I saw it.

A faint green glow near the trees.

It began like mist, barely visible—then thickened, deepened, shaped itself into presence.

Akshara.

She didn't float gently this time.

She rushed toward me, fast and urgent, her aura flaring violently, green shot through with panic. Her face was tight, eyes wide—not playful, not teasing.

Terrified.

"Lee," she said quickly, words colliding. "There is a fourth person. I finally understood it."

I stood up instantly.

My heartbeat changed—hard, alert.

"Slow down," I said, though my body already knew. "Explain."

She took a breath—not to calm herself, but to think faster.

"Dinesh came to that house before everything started," she said. "Before the plan. Before the trafficking. He went there like it was normal."

My stomach tightened.

"He stopped coming after they began," she continued. "Completely. Like he didn't want his presence recorded anymore."

I nodded slowly.

The pattern was forming.

"Juicy knows only three," Akshara said. "Because the fourth came later. Stayed outside. Watched. Protected himself."

My jaw clenched.

"The constable was right," I said. "There were four."

Akshara nodded—but she wasn't finished.

Her voice dropped when she spoke again.

"Kiran got the letter because he was my boyfriend."

Everything stopped.

For one full second, my body forgot how to breathe.

"We kept it private," she added softly. "Even you didn't know."

She was right.

I hadn't.

And suddenly the truth sharpened brutally.

On her side, only two people knew.

Me.

And him.

I looked at her.

"You never told anyone," I said slowly. "So the only way they knew… is if Kiran told someone."

Akshara turned away.

Her glow flickered.

"I didn't want to believe it," she whispered. "But everything points to him."

Silence fell.

Not empty.

Heavy.

The kind that changes you.

"It's late," I said finally. "We'll talk to him tomorrow."

But even as I said it, I knew—

Fear doesn't wait.

Truth doesn't wait.

If Akshara was right, every minute mattered.

I made the call.

An MBBS friend.

Then another.

"Where does Kiran live?"

The address came in seconds.

I stood up.

"I'm going now."

Akshara didn't stop me.

She only nodded.

***

Kiran's House

Kiran's house looked ordinary.

Too ordinary.

A neat gate.

Clean porch.

Warm lights inside.

A life continuing.

As if nothing had happened.

As if a girl hadn't been destroyed.

I knocked.

When Kiran opened the door and saw me—

Shock.

Not happiness.

Not irritation.

Shock.

Like he was seeing someone who wasn't supposed to exist.

"Lee?" he said.

Thin voice.

Akshara stood beside me, staring at him.

No rage.

Only betrayal.

"Can I come in?" I asked.

Pause.

Calculation.

“Yes.”

Inside smelled of coffee and detergent.

Clean. Organized. Perfect.

Family photos lined the wall.

Smiling faces.

I sat.

“What happened that night?” I asked calmly.

Kiran rubbed his forehead—rehearsed fatigue.

“We went to a pub,” he said. “Music. Alcohol. We enjoyed.”

“She suddenly fell asleep.”

Akshara stiffened.

“I never fall asleep like that,” she said quietly.

I watched him closely.

Every blink.

Every pause.

“Where are your wife and children?” I asked.

“At school,” he said too quickly.

He stood.

“Coffee?”

He didn’t wait.

The cup was placed in my hand.

Warm. Bitter.

“I dropped her near her house,” he said. “Rang the bell. Left.”

Akshara’s aura trembled.

“I remember the gate,” she whispered. “Not the bell.”

I looked up.

"Did her parents come out?"

One second.

Just one.

"No."

That was enough.

The cup slipped from my hand.

Shattered.

The world tilted.

My heartbeat slowed—not fear.

Poison.

My legs failed.

I collapsed.

As darkness closed in, the last things I saw were—

Akshara, her green aura flaring violently, glass cracking beside her.

And Kiran—

standing over me.

Not panicked.

Not helping.

Just watching.

Waiting.

Chapter - 20
The Truths (Continued)

AKSHARA

Sunday, January 8 — Evening

The Park

Moonlight lay gently across the park, turning every flower pale silver, every shadow soft at the edges. The lights Lee had once installed glowed quietly along the path—steady, patient, as if they had been waiting for this moment all along.

Lee sat on the bench, shoulders lowered, breath uneven. The strength he carried so easily in daylight had abandoned him here. He looked like a man who had survived everything—except goodbye.

I stood beside him, watching his face. The lines of pain. The exhaustion. The love he never tried to hide anymore.

For a while, neither of us spoke.

Then I tilted my head slightly and said, almost playfully—trying to steal his sadness for just one moment,

"Do you want to see me… as I was? As a human?"

He turned toward me instantly, startled, hope flickering in his eyes like a match struck in darkness.

"Yes," he said. "Please."

Something warm passed through me.

Not blood.

Not breath.

But something close enough to both.

"Close your eyes," I said softly.

He did.

I hesitated for just a second.

"Do you remember my face?" I asked quietly.

He didn't pause. Didn't search his memory.

"I never forget," he said.

That was when something inside me broke open—something gentle.

"Okay," I whispered. "Then imagine this."

I slowed my words, dressing myself again inside his mind.

"Imagine a traditional pink top dress," I said, smiling to myself. "Soft fabric. Half-quartered puffed sleeves. The kind I loved but never wore often."

His breathing changed.

"And a cream off-white lehanga," I continued, "decorated with golden and multicolored embroidered motifs. Not heavy. Not flashy. Just… beautiful."

I was about to say more—

When Lee spoke.

Slowly.

Confidently.

Like he was seeing me clearly.

"Your eyes are sharp," he said. "Not aggressive. Just honest. Like they notice everything."

My aura trembled.

"Your black hair moves with the air," he continued. "Not controlled. Just free."

I felt something like breathing—even though I wasn't.

"No jewelry," he said softly. "You never liked it. Just one bracelet on your right hand."

I smiled.

"And your hands are covered with mehndi," he added. "Still dark. Still fresh."

His voice softened further.

"You're not hot," he said gently. "You're endlessly cute. Beautiful in a way that doesn't try."

Tears blurred his closed eyes.

"And when you smile… your cheeks move first."

That was it.

For the first time since my death, I understood something fully.

This is how true love feels.

Not possession.

Not desire.

Recognition.

I felt beautiful—not because of how I looked, but because of how I was seen.

For a moment, I forgot I was already gone.

I didn't want to leave him.

But fate doesn't care what you want.

Lee opened his eyes.

The glow around me had thinned. My edges were softening.

"It's time," I said quietly.

His face changed instantly. Panic. Denial. Pain.

"No," he whispered.

He raised his hand.

So did I.

Our palms moved toward each other—slowly, desperately.

They passed through.

Nothing touched.

Everything hurt.

I smiled through it.

"Live well," I said softly. "That's how you keep me."

His lips trembled.

"I love you," he said.

"I know," I replied. "I always knew."

And then I stepped back.

The Forest

Mist hung low between the trees, thick and cold, like breath trapped between worlds. The forest felt older than language—quiet in a way that demanded respect.

The rishi stood at the center of the clearing.

Putri was there too.

She smiled brightly when she saw me. “Hi.”

The rishi lifted his hand.

“No,” he said firmly. “You made a soul.”

Putri fell silent.

I stepped into the circle and sat at its center. The ground beneath me felt neither solid nor empty—just waiting.

The rishi opened his mouth. Ancient words poured out, heavy with authority.

As the ritual began, regret flooded me.

I thought of my parents.

I’m sorry, Amma. I’m sorry, Nanna.

I thought of Lee.

I’m sorry I can’t be with you in this life.

And with everything I had left, I prayed—not for myself—

But for him.

Let him be happy.

Let him love freely.

Let his life be gentle.

Light wrapped around me.

Not violently.

I was swallowed—not eaten, not destroyed—absorbed.

My name thinned.

My memories loosened.

And then—

There was nothing.

Akshara was no more.

Chapter - 21
The End

LEE

Sunday, January 8 — 4:00 P.M.

I watched her aura drift away.

It didn't disappear like smoke.

It didn't vanish like a flame being blown out.

It simply… became lighter.

Thinner.

Like a piece of the sky peeling itself away from the world and returning to where it belonged.

For a few seconds, I didn't move at all.

I sat frozen on the bench, my eyes fixed on the empty air where she had been—waiting, stupidly, desperately—for her glow to return. As if grief could be reversed by staring hard enough. As if love could pull the dead back into form.

But the light kept fading.

The green softened into pale mist.

The mist thinned into nothing.

And then—she was gone.

The park remained.

The flowers remained.

The bench remained.

Only she didn't.

Something sharp tightened around my throat, burning like I had swallowed fire. My chest felt too small for my lungs, as if the air itself refused to enter me properly. I tried to speak—just one word, just one sound—

Please… don't leave me.

But my voice failed.

It always did.

Every time I needed it most, it disappeared—like courage does when it finally meets truth.

My hands trembled slightly, resting on my knees. I stared at my fingers as if they belonged to another man. The doctor in me knew exactly what heartbreak did to the body—pulse rising, muscles tensing, breath failing—but the boy inside me didn't care about science.

He only wanted her back.

This park—

This entire place—

I hadn't built it as a business idea.

I hadn't built it for reputation.

I hadn't even built it to feel good.

I had built it because I couldn't undo her death.

Every brick here was guilt.

Every pathway was apology.

Every light was a prayer I never knew how to say out loud.

I remembered how she used to joke about my seriousness.

"Lee," she once said, rolling her eyes, "if you keep walking like this, even trees will feel judged."

I had smiled then—barely.

Now that memory hurt more than silence.

I stayed in the park for a long time.

Not because I wanted to.

But because my body refused to stand up and leave her behind.

The entire place felt like a grave that had been forced to grow flowers.

I stared at the soft lights lining the path, the glow reflecting gently on petals. A park built from regret still smelled beautiful.

That was the cruelest part.

Every memory replayed itself.

Akshara laughing when she teased me.

Akshara glaring at me when her rage escaped control.

Akshara falling silent when words failed her.

Akshara turning white, blue, red—like her soul spoke in colors because human language was never enough.

And then her final voice—

The way she said *Alena loves you*.

The way she said it like her last gift to me.

The way she admitted jealousy without bitterness.

The way she still worried about my future while her own was ending.

I remembered how she tried to touch me at the end.

Her hand had passed through mine.

She had smiled sadly and whispered,

"See? Even now… I miss being human."

That sentence broke something permanent inside me.

When I finally stood up, my legs felt weak.

But my heart felt heavier.

I walked slowly along the path, touching nothing, disturbing nothing—like the park itself might collapse if I moved too fast. The flowers swayed gently, and for one foolish second, I imagined her standing among them again, arms crossed, smirking.

"Don't look so dramatic," she would have said.

"I'm not dying twice for you."

But it was only the wind.

Only the leaves.

Only emptiness.

***

That Night

I couldn't sleep.

The house felt wrong—too quiet. Not peaceful quiet. Empty quiet. The kind that makes your own breathing feel loud and misplaced.

I sat on my bed staring at the wall until my eyes burned. Then I stared at my phone until my fingers moved without permission.

On impulse, I messaged Alena.

Are you coming tomorrow?

Her reply came instantly.

Yes.

My throat tightened—not with grief this time, but with something fragile and unfamiliar.

Hope.

Can I talk to you? I typed.

Her reply came again.

You don't need permission.

I read that sentence again and again.

Like proof that life hadn't ended with death.

Like permission to exist again.

***

The Next Morning

For the first time in years, I dressed not like a man hiding behind formality—but like someone ready to live.

A plain white T-shirt.

White cargo pants.

A sky-blue coat.

Nothing expensive.

Nothing cold.

Nothing meant to intimidate.

Just clean. Simple. Honest.

I looked into the mirror once—not to admire.

To confirm.

This is me now.

I picked up roses on the way.

Traffic slowed everything down like always, but for once I didn't curse it. Rushing had only brought darkness into my life before.

Today, I wanted calm hands.

At the hospital, people stared. Some out of respect. Some out of fear.

I ignored all of it.

Alena was already in the cafeteria.

She wore a black T-shirt and jeans—simple, comfortable. Her hair was loosely tied. Her eyes were tired.

When she saw me, hope flickered across her face.

I handed her the flowers.

She didn't accept them like a rich man's gesture.

She held them like proof she mattered.

I sat down immediately.

"Please," I said softly. "Don't speak for five minutes."

She nodded.

And waited.

I told her everything that mattered.

Not the ghost.

Not the violence.

Just the truth.

"I love you," I said finally. "And I'm done running from that."

When I asked her if she loved me, she teased me first—because that was her nature.

Then she said yes.

And held my hand.

Real.

Warm.

Alive.

Later—quietly, without drama—I proposed.

No crowd.

No knees.

No spectacle.

Just honesty.

She cried.

Then laughed.

Then said yes again—just to be sure.

***

Years Later

The park was brighter than I remembered.

Full of footsteps.

Children's laughter.

Life.

I stood behind my little daughter, Akshara, watching her take her first unsteady steps.

Her legs wobbled.

Her arms stretched for balance.

She giggled.

And then she walked.

Lee didn't breathe.

He moved toward her and knelt immediately, eyes shining, hands open.

But she stopped.

Right in front of a flower.

She crouched clumsily and touched the petals.

Parijatham.

Night jasmine.

The same flower Akshara had loved.

My eyes burned.

Not with pain.

With recognition.

"She liked this flower," I whispered.

"She was called Akshara too."

The wind carried jasmine through the park.

And for the first time—

It didn't feel like loss.

It felt like continuity.

Some loves never leave.

They just change form.

And this time—

I was not going to waste what was left.